DOPE BOY MAGIC

Chris Green

Lock Down Publications and Ca$h Presents
Dope Boy Magic
A Novel by *Chris Green*

Chris Green

Lock Down Publications
P.O. Box 870494
Mesquite, Tx 75187

Visit our website @
www.lockdownpublications.com

First Edition December 2019
Printed in the United States of America

Lock Down Publications
Like our page on Facebook: Lock Down Publications @
www.facebook.com/lockdownpublications.ldp
Cover design and layout by: **Dynasty Cover Me**
Book interior design by: **Shawn Walker**
Edited by: **Lashonda Johnson**

4

Stay Connected with Us!

Text **LOCKDOWN** to 22828 to stay up-to-date with new releases, sneak peaks, contests and more…

Thank you.

Submission Guideline.

Submit the first three chapters of your completed manuscript to ldpsubmissions@gmail.com, subject line: Your book's title. The manuscript must be in a .doc file and sent as an attachment. Document should be in Times New Roman, double spaced and in size 12 font. Also, provide your synopsis and full contact information. If sending multiple submissions, they must each be in a separate email.

Have a story but no way to send it electronically? You can still submit to LDP/Ca$h Presents. Send in the first three chapters, written or typed, of your completed manuscript to:

LDP: Submissions Dept
Po Box 870494
Mesquite, Tx 75187

DO NOT send original manuscript. Must be a duplicate.

Provide your synopsis and a cover letter containing your full contact information.

Thanks for considering LDP and Ca$h Presents.

Acknowledgements

As always, my mother Dolsellia is the reason for me being this prudent individual. I respect that I have a queen who will stand by me at any cost. You are the reason I push, you and my daughter. My big brother, D'Lo, my little brothers, Nation and Wild. Without you guys, I'm just a man. With you all, I'm Chris the smart, spontaneous and adventurous person that everyone loves.

Shoutout to LDP, Cash, Shawn and everyone else that's pushing our movement. Of course, I love you guys whether we bond or not. This is a new level to my life and it's going to take some time to get intact.

Last but not least, my readers. You guys are so wonderful. I admire you all. always know that your love and support is the best. Hopefully, you all will enjoy this new art that I took my time to work on.

Peace

Chris Green

Prologue

July 29, 2008

After easing down the staircase, Tipton made his way through the dark living room and into the kitchen. It was the same routine every Friday. A cooking school for his mother's workers who didn't know the first rules on whipping that dope.

Mary White better known as Queen of the City moved through Augusta and Atlanta, Ga as if she'd wrote the mayor a million-dollar check to watch her bricks drop harder than a crack head's baby. Not only was she the best, but her skills would have the average Money Mitch ass nigga working back at the cleaners with Ace. Her low-cut Toni Braxton hairstyle complimented her brown eyes and plump backside. Nothing touched her body, but the best designer fabrics and her brown peanut butter skin would drive the richest nigga out of his Mercedes Benz.

As she balanced the Pyrex pot in her hand, she glanced over at her son who was posted with an inquisitive eye. "Tip, I thought I told you Fridays are off-limits?"

"And you also said you was gonna teach me, mama," he replied, tired of being turned away.

Observing the ten keys that sat on the glass table, Tip smiled. His mind was eager to follow his Queen's ambition.

"Come here." She grinned standing by the stove.

Once he made his way over, Mary handed him the glass pot and spoon. Before she could give him the steps, he began twisting his wrist like a ten-year veteran.

She looked back at her workers and smiled. "I guess it just runs in his blood."

Hearing the doorbell ring, Mary motioned for one of her men to answer it, while observing her son grow inside her family business.

"Remember when you start seeing it lock up, splash a little cold water with your fingers and keep flicking, baby boy."

Hearing the loud semi-automatic gunshots rang out Mary grabbed Tipton and pushed him behind her. The second guard quickly reached for his weapon and prepared to stand up. Before he could rise from the chair. One masked man entered the kitchen and placed two shots to his chest.

Boc! Boc!

The gun burped loudly causing Mary to jump from the sight of blood splattering over her eating table. Two more men entered behind him with heavy assault rifles. Their eyes landed on the prize that was stacked on top of the thick glass.

"Just take it and leave!" Mary shook while holding Tipton.

As the two men began bagging up the product, one of the masked robbers moved closer. "If I lose, you lose," he spat with malice in his tone before raising the gun to her forehead.

Realizing who was standing in front of her, the flash and bang erupted sending a slug directly through the center of her skull.

Boc!

After watching his mother fall to the floor, Tipton fell beside her. "Ma," his whimpers were low before tears filled his eyes.

Standing before him with his gun still smoking, the killer turned to leave. The last thing Tipton's eyes spotted was the cursive L, tattooed on the man's wrist, as he made his way out of the house with the two goons behind him. Tipton shook uncontrollably before releasing a wretched scream. His young heart couldn't process the action that took place right before his eyes. That was a thirteenth birthday he would never be able to forget.

Chapter 1

Three Years Later

After hearing the alarm clock blare on top of his dresser, Tipton's auntie invaded his room at the same time she did every morning.

"It's time to get yo ass up and get to school, nigga! I told you I don't need these motherfuckers blowing me up while I'm at work talking about how many days you've missed," her voice was always a little too loud.

Tipton rolled from under his cover and stared at her with hatred in his eyes. Her filthy ass robe looked like someone buried it inside a trash can. Her shirt was too little, exposing her tiger-striped belly and the stinky smell of her wood tip black and mild filled the room.

"Tip, please don't make me slap yo' face straight boy. And I'ma need some motherfucking co-pay for all these junkie ass teenagers knocking on my damn door early in the a.m. for some fucking weed. You got thirty minutes to be out of my house," she said with a serious tone before leaving him be.

Shaking his head in silence, Tip stretched and headed for his personal bathroom. He walked in and cut on the light observing himself in the mirror. Tipton Devon White was originally born in Detroit, Michigan after his mother left New Orleans on the run for a parole violation. While working a regular nine to five job, she realized five hundred bucks every two weeks just wasn't the way she wanted to feed her one and only child. After networking and meeting a few new cats who was willing to cash out on a bad bitch, Mary packed her things and headed straight for the city of opportunity, Atlanta.

It didn't take long for her to settle in because, by the age of three, Tipton didn't want for anything. After stepping into the dope game, Mary met a plug who'd teach her something that would change her life forever and that was how to cook dope.

Her first few times was a stumble, but figuring out that she could turn one to two and two to four, Mary became one of the baddest bitches to ever touch a Pyrex pot. It was never known how much money Mary was truly sitting on. Most knew it ranged in the millions, but her business was always kept on the hush. She'd carried Atlanta on her back for so long, that everyone changed after finding out she was murdered in her own home. Still to this day, no one knew who'd pulled the treacherous stunt, but slick statements would be heard sliding through the air.

Splashing the water across his face, he rubbed a hand through his deep waves. Standing 5'10 with a medium build, Tipton didn't favor the average sixteen-year-old. His low, light-brown eyes and smooth, talking skills was the golden ticket for all the young horny females. Not to mention, he wouldn't go a day without adding more numbers to his bankroll. In everyone's eyes, he was just a guy who could do no wrong. He was never arrogant, or flashy. His demeanor was quiet and humble, but it definitely wasn't a characteristic everyone took lightly.

After being sent to a juvenile detention center for beating a teenager so bad he had a seizure, his popularity rose to the top at West Lake High School. A trait he just couldn't leave alone was hustling. Even though Mary left him a huge check with his uncle, it was paper he couldn't touch until he turned eighteen. After finding a weed plug on the Northside of Gwinnett County, he purchased a pound of weed and never looked back. The connect wasn't used to seeing a kid so young move two pounds a week. It eventually doubled to four, allowing him to average a cool seven-grand every two weeks.

After jumping in the shower, he climbed out and got dressed. He slipped on a pair of crispy 504 *Levi* jeans, tossed a fitted white tee shirt over his body and threw on the brand-new pair of *Lebron* sneakers he purchased the day before. Then he stuffed two ounces of marijuana into his pocket, grabbed five hundred bucks out of the *Nike* shoebox and headed out of his room.

As he trailed through the living area, his auntie rose from the couch and blocked the front door. "Nigga you must've thought I was playing. Co-pay before your ass comes home to an eviction notice." She mugged with her hand out.

"Lisa, I'm not a little boy. Watch how you talk to me," he replied smoothly pulling a c-note out of his pocket and placing it in her palm.

"Whatever! That's ya problem, you think ya grown. My house—my rules."

When she took her seat back in front of the television, Tipton shook his head before walking out. Even though Lisa wasn't his blood aunt, he still showed her respect on the strength of being one of his mother's best friends. Accepting him into her home was something he truly valued. Including the push, she always gave him about going to school. It showed through all the nagging and annoyance that she really did care.

He jumped in his 2007 Dodge Charger and skated out of the parking lot. Unlike most young niggas who was riding around in a junkie rental, Tipton was licensed with his own shit. It wasn't the latest upgrade, but he was grateful that riding a Marta bus wasn't an option. It was hard trying to make a living in the city. Habits and addictions were bound to take you to a place of no return. Only the ones with a passion for grinding and stacking would rise to the top and eat. Settling for less was something that the young hustler's ambition wouldn't allow.

It was twenty-five minutes later when he pulled into the high school driveway. *Young Jeezy's* song *'Hypnotized,'* blared through the speakers causing numerous heads to turn. Killing his engine, Tipton got out of his whip and walked directly into the path of his homeroom teacher.

"Mr. White, you know that loud music isn't allowed on school property, right?" Ms. Berrett was a dark-skinned woman who wore her clothes tight as insect pussy. She had what everyone would call a big ma duke booty. Her kitty print was on swole 24/7 and her hair was always braided to the back. If she didn't wear her glasses, it would be hard to tell that she was in her thirties.

"The music wasn't loud, Ms. Berrett. My speakers just don't know how to act." He winked his eye.

Blushing, she looked him up and down before heading for the entrance. "Learn to follow the rules, Mr. White."

Heading inside, Tipton moved in a hurry to the second cafeteria. When he opened the door, the loud commotion was like music to his ears. Everybody moved about their way until one of his homies called his name.

"Yo', Tip!" Rex yelled as if he wasn't the loudest nigga in the cafeteria.

It didn't take long for all the young teenagers to see that he was in the building. Instantly, they bum-rushed him with twenties and fifties in hand for the strong chronic that they could smell coming from his jeans.

Wasting no time, he pulled out a zip of premium and served as if he was in front of Campbellton Road's Stop n Shop corner store. Before he could sit down at the table, an entire ounce was sold, and his pockets was three hundred dollars fatter.

"Damn, nigga! Did you at least save us one blunt?" Rex asked seeing the crowd walk away with the huge gram sacks of weed.

"Did you wear any pants to school today?" he replied sarcastically giving his partna some dap.

Rex was more of a comedian. He loved to make everybody laugh. Standing 6'2 in height, he was the tallest and skinniest teen in the eleventh grade. His dreads were always wrapped up in case a basketball game ever presented itself. And most of his money always went to Tipton because he couldn't live without smoking weed.

"Hey Tip!" A young chic greeted, stepping in front of him.

Looking up in her face, he yawned. "Wassup, Chocolate?"

"Shit! I was just wondering if you pulling up to my house party tonight or what?" she asked with a mouth full of bubble gum.

Shaking his ear thinking that he heard wrong, Tipton chuckled. "You throwing a house party? Yo' mama must've taken a trip to Hawaii or something?"

"Nah, she staying with her boyfriend for the weekend and I got the house to myself. It's gonna be lit and you know we need a weed man, so you need to drop through.

Thinking on it for a second, Tipton nodded. "I'll slide over for a little bit."

"Cool, I guess I'll see you tonight." She smiled as she walked off.

"Nigga why you be slick dissing, Chocolate? That girl be sweating the shit out of you?" Rex said as she exited the cafeteria.

"That's the point, she be sweating a little too hard, which means she wants something. Unfortunately, I'm not able to assist her with nothing. Where's, Dejuan?"

"Man, you know that nigga been bucking on coming to school for the past few days. He keeps kicking that shit 'bout he gotta get some money or whatever."

"Bet, I need to scream at both of y'all about something important. I guess we can wait until we slide through this party tonight," Tipton said then glanced at the time on his cellphone.

"Smooth," Rex responded. "Let's go ahead and get to class so we can get this day over with."

****

It was close to the bell ringing and the day was dragging by like it would never end. Waiting to put his plan together, Tipton plotted as he watched the long hand on the clock touch thirty. Hearing the bell sound for their release, everyone jumped from their seats as if a fire had broken out.

"Remember, you will receive an F on the project if this report is not completed by Monday. Mr. White, I need you to stay back so I can speak to you please," Ms. Berrett announced before he could walk out.

Taking a deep breath, Tipton stopped in his tracks.

"What the hell did you do?" Rex whispered letting his classmates move pass him.

Shrugging his shoulders with a clueless expression, Tipton sat back down.

"Give me seven grams of that gas and I'll beat that bitch like I was, Terrence Howard on Hustle and Flow," Rex mumbled in his ear.

Trying not to laugh, Tipton placed a hand over his mouth.

"Mr. Johnson, he will see you in the parking lot," Ms. Berrett said with a stern tone.

Rex laughed and made his way out of the classroom, shutting the door behind him.

"Tipton, could you step up to my desk please?"

Sensing she was about to question him on the recent days of school he missed. He decided to go ahead and let her rant, so he could make it out of the school building in a timely fashion.

"Yes, Ma'am?"

"Step around here next to me and look at this paper, please," she said while looking into his low brown eyes.

Moving around to the other side of her desk, Tipton stared down at the absent slot on his calendar.

"Is there any reason you missed five days of school?"

"I think I was sick if I'm not mistaking," he lied.

She turned her rolling chair towards him and Tipton tried his best not to stare at the monkey bulging in her pants. "Lies don't care who tell them, Tipton. I guess if I reach in your pocket, I wouldn't find that weed I keep smelling either?"

Catching him off guard with her statement, Tipton stuttered. He was guaranteed to get kicked out of school with a huge felony if he got caught with the ounce he was toting. Seeing her hand move toward him, Tipton knew the cops was surely about to be called. His mind instantly froze, as she grabbed the top of his zipper and slid it down slowly. She kept her gaze on him, slid his manhood from his pants and placed a delicate kiss on the head. Then quickly downed him in her mouth, his teacher gagged, as he touched the back of her throat.

Tipton stared in amazement with his mouth ajar, she bobbed her head back and forth, soaking his dick with her explosive tongue game. She used her free hand, dug inside his pocket and pulled out the marijuana. She removed four large sacks, placed it back inside his jeans and finished her job. She deep-throated him twice, causing him to release his juices all over her warm lips.

After swallowing his drink, she fixed his pants with a wide smile. "Make sure you bring yo' ass to school. You never know what you could learn boy."

As the older woman stood up from her seat, he stared at her juicy ass. "You're full of surprises, Ms. Berrett. I swear it feels like I'm missing something," he replied, grabbing a handful of her booty.

"You gotta another two months before you take that course young man, seventeen or better." She winked, before opening the classroom door.

"Can I at least know how good I did on my test?"

"A-plus." She grinned seductively, closing the door behind him.

As he walked down the hallway, Tipton couldn't help but laugh. Maybe school wasn't as bad as he thought.

Chris Green

Chapter 2

It was around eight in the evening when Tipton, Rex, and Dejuan pulled in front of Chocolate's crib. Teenagers roamed in as if her shit was the known trap spot. All it was gonna take was one nosy ass neighbor to realize her mama wasn't home, and all hell was gonna break loose.

The trio climbed out of Tipton's whip and headed inside. "What was it you wanted to talk about, fool?" Dejuan questioned, as they walked up the driveway.

"I'll pour y'all a cup after we leave here. It shouldn't take that long."

Nodding, they made their way through the front door. Tipton was surprised to see that Chocolate kept her word. Shit was definitely live. The living room was so packed you could barely see who was in the building.

"Oh, fuck yeah. I'm 'bout to go dance with like thirty of those dirty panty hoes." Rex smiled before walking towards the crowd.

"Don't get lost, I don't plan on being here that long," Tipton stated.

"I'm 'bout to slide to this bitch bathroom real quick. I'll be right back," Dejuan said disappearing behind Rex.

As he posted against the wall, Tipton saluted a couple of niggas he knew from school and served a few people who was in need of some pressure.

After vibing to the loud music for a second, Chocolate made her way across the room toward him. "Wassup, Tip? Why the hell you ain't out there on the dance floor?"

"I don't dance, I just nod lil' mama."

Chocolate laughed at his remark, his eyes happened to turn to the left landing on a caramel bunny. "Who the fuck is that?" he asked pointing a finger.

Turning her attention in the direction he faced, Chocolate sucked her teeth. "That's just my fucking cousin, Peaches."

Tipton was star struck, shorty's ass sat on her back like a pumpkin. The gold streaks in her hair matched her pretty skin tone. The tattoos that covered her right arm and leg made her appearance even more provocative.

"I want her," he mouthed with a look as if he was ready to attack her.

"Boy, my cousin is too old for you. She's twenty-one, Tip," Chocolate said with envy in her tone.

"I wouldn't give a damn if she was twenty-nine. Tell her to bring her ass here."

"And what do I get out of the deal?" she asked folding her arms across her breasts.

Tipton pulled a gram of weed from his pocket, opened the top of her shirt and stuffed it into her bra. "Go handle that."

She smiled and moved across the room, as he leaned back against the wall. He watched Chocolate work her mojo as Peaches looked over at Tipton with a slight smirk. It didn't take long before she was moving closer to him with her soft butt quaking from side to side.

"*Bring yo' ass here* is not the way you talk to a lady. Where's your manners?" she asked standing back on her legs.

Now that she was up close, Tipton knew she was a dime piece for sure. "You're right, but I talk to *my lady* like that. Now bring yo' ass here."

Peaches cheesed, showing her two gold teeth at the bottom of her mouth. "How old are you?" She gazed up and down at his swag.

"I'm sixteen, but my bankroll feels like I'm forty and about to retire."

"*Sixteen!* What do you really think you can do with all this? I'll drive you crazy."

"Not if I can beat you to it," he replied, showing his dimples.

"I hear you. When can I find out, Mr. Good Talker?" Peaches giggled looking into his brown eyes.

Tipton pulled out his cell phone and placed it in her hand. "I'll come and pick you up tomorrow if you're not too busy."

Peaches placed her digits in the phone, slid it back into his pocket and gently kissed his lips. "Be careful what you wish foe youngin'," Peaches whispered before sliding off.

As he watched her ass move like it had a mind of its own, Tipton knew she was his.

"God-damn! Who the fuck is that?" Rex asked, catching the end of their conversation.

"Hopefully my new wife."

"Bruh, I'll stab my fucking mama to get in between a soft ass like that."

Tipton laughed, shaking his head. "You fucking stupid man. Where the hell is, Dejuan?"

"He in one of those bedrooms smashing, Chocolate."

"Stop lying."

"Bruh, I'ma Christian, you know we only lie at church," Rex confirmed with a serious face.

Before Tipton could debate, Dejaun protruded from the back of the house. While he made his way across the living room floor, sweat ran down his forehead and a cigarette rested between his lips, as he approached them.

"I'm ready."

"Was it good?" Tipton asked with a raised brow.

"Shawty a freak," he responded walking out the front door.

"I told you." Rex laughed, as they headed out behind him.

****

After rolling a few blunts, Tipton got out of the car and walked inside the house. "My auntie might say something. Just keep walking to the room," he whispered to Rex and Dejuan, as they moved through the quiet living room.

Just as he suspected, Lisa opened her bedroom door. "Tip, what the hell do you think you doing? This ain't no house party up in this motherfucker."

"We just gonna talk for a little while and head right back out. It's no big deal," he answered calmly.

"Ain't none of them niggas you hang with paying no bills or fucking me, co-pay, nigga."

Grabbing the bridge of his nose, Tipton pulled four twenty-dollar bills from his back pocket. "It's mighty funny that nasty ass nigga who laying in yo' bed can't toss you twenty dollars."

"Motherfucker, this my—"

Before Lisa could finish ranting, Tipton walked into his room and slammed the door behind him. "Bruh, your auntie looks like one of those slaves from the Amistad. She be complaining but you can't ever understand what she saying," Rex joked, forcing Dejuan to laugh loudly.

"Shut the fuck up man. I'm really ready to get my own shit. I'm tired of dealing with her." Tipton sparked one of the rolled blunts.

"Why don't you go ahead and do it? You really do need some space, my nigga."

"That's the reason I needed to talk to y'all," Tipton said inhaling on the weed.

"So, wassup?" Dejuan asked impatiently.

"I been knowing y'all boys for over three years now. I don't trust niggas period, but I been planning this for a minute. I need y'all help with hustling this weed," he confirmed looking back and forth between them.

"Bruh, you don't need no help doing shit. You been hustling fine by yourself since we met you. It ain't never been hard for you to get off a few bags my guy," Rex spoke before grabbing the blunt.

"I ain't talking about no two bags and if I didn't need help, I wouldn't have asked."

"How much you talking about?" Dejuan chimed in.

Tipton stood up, opened his closet and removed a large black garbage bag. He took the knot out of the top and poured the contents on the bed.

"Damn, bro. What you been doing, growing this shit?" Rex picked up a compressed bag and pressed it against his nose.

"My plug out North is really messing with my campaign. I pulled up on him last week and he sold me twenty of them for cheap. The way I see it, we can break it down and make a killing. Or we could get rid of it wholesale and double up."

"It wouldn't matter how you do it. You still gon' eat," Rex stated.

"Nah, *we* gon' eat regardless. Like I said, I don't trust people, but y'all my boys. If this shit go right on the first run, we can take it to another level and lock all this shit down. I just need one thing from both of y'all." Tipton sat back down.

"What's that?" Dejuan asked.

"Stay low key because that flashy stuff brings two things out. The jack boys and the police and I don't feel like seeing neither one. Second, I need y'all to vow that we never let this money shit come between us."

"You got my word, bro. I love y'all niggas like fat girls love cookies." Rex sparked another joint.

"Dejuan?" Tipton watched, as he stared at the weed.

"I've been in since day one, you know I'm with it," he answered after snapping out of his trance.

"That's all I need to hear," Tipton smirked before leaning back with the wheels turning in his head.

Chris Green

Chapter 3

"Ooohhh shit, Daddy!" Peaches moaned as Tipton eased in her from the back.

As he stared at the huge butterfly on her cheeks, he plunged harder. Her booty was soft like tissue and he tried his best to contain it in between his fingers. Her Kitty farted in delight from his length. Peaches arched her back deeper and Tipton slow stroked his manhood back and forth in her goodies. She looked back at him and began slamming her backside against his pelvis, then his orgasm erupted inside of her.

The second he pulled out Peaches turned around and placed him into her mouth. After two minutes of her experienced mouth game, Tipton was back rock solid.

Peaches turned on her side and raised her right leg exposing her sweet spot. "Give me more of my dick," she teased bouncing her butt cheek.

Knowing that a call-out couldn't be denied, he climbed back on the bed and put his work in for the next hour. Afterward, Peaches laid in his arms and slowly fell into a deep sleep. Tipton's mind couldn't help but ponder on how he'd bagged her fine ass. Her sex was official, but her motives were still unclear. Tipton wanted something serious, a relationship that could last forever. His heart was built on getting cheddar but being around his mother and growing up without a father taught him how to truly love. In the end, he just prayed she was ready to be a wife and not another piece of ass.

Moving from under her arms, Tipton wrapped the sheet around her and slid on his Nike sweats. When he walked out of his room, Lisa stood in her doorway with a huge frown.

"*Ooo, Daddy, yeah baby,*" she mimicked Peaches in a low tone while looking at Tipton.

Tipton folded his arms and stared at her with a pathetic expression.

"You fucking bitches in my house and shit? I need some motherfucking—"

"Copay, right?" he finished off her sentence before she could.

"Exactly, now you catching on."

Realizing he would never be able to get around Lisa without having to come out of his pocket, Tipton officially made up his mind, it was time to move out. It had been three weeks since he added Rex and Dejuan to his game plan and shit was flowing lovely. Not only were they supplying the entire school, but the numbers on the street was sitting pretty. Within that little time, Tipton saved over ninety grand. Not including what he had in work. In his mind, he didn't need shit from Lisa.

"Fuck yo' co-pay, I'll be out of your house in the next thirty minutes." He walked back into his room.

"Yeah, right boy, you ain't got nowhere to go!" Lisa yelled as he shut the door.

"Hey, Shorty, wake up," he whispered kissing Peaches on her cheek.

"Wassup, Daddy, do I gotta leave?" She stirred from her sleep quickly.

"Nah, we about to leave," he said before walking into his bathroom.

Peaches sat up in the bed and watched him move hastily. "What's wrong, did I get you in trouble or something?"

"Nah, you Gucci. It's been time for me to slide out this motherfucker anyway. How fast can you get us an apartment?" He walked back over to her.

"I mean, it depends on what you want. I'm plugged in with some people who own some townhomes on the Northside. I would have to pay a deposit and—"

"Here, that's seven racks. Get us a spot asap. Pay whatever it cost, I can take care of the rest when we move in," he interrupted her while tossing on his kicks.

"Daddy, I got a little money saved, I can help you."

"I didn't ask for help, I said get us a crib. Tell them you'll pay the first three months' rent if we can move in today."

She lowered her head and nodded.

Then he leaned over the bed and placed a kiss on her lips. "No frowns, we don't get mad because we too busy being happy. You're my lady, so let ya man do his job okay?" He grabbed her chin, so she could look into his eyes.

"Okay, baby." She grinned, before jumping on her phone to handle the business.

Even though he'd only known Peaches for a month, grown men made grown decisions and it was officially time to grow up. After she placed the call and received the confirmation that they were all set, he began tossing all his important belongings in a garbage bag.

"Go ahead and jump in the shower real quick. By the time you're done, I'll be ready." He opened the bedroom door.

He carried the bags to his car and placed the stash in the back of his trunk under the spare tire. He moved over to Peaches' Malibu and threw a bag of clothes and the large supply into her backseat. Heading back in the house to gather his things, Lisa stood at the door with anger pumping through her skull.

"Nigga, you stupid. You think just 'cause you got a little hustle going on, you can make it in those streets? If you leave out of my house, you better not come back." Lisa tapped her foot repeatedly like a miserable old woman.

"I won't," he replied calmly, before sliding back to his room. By the time he finished gathering the rest of his things. Peaches was getting out of the shower.

"Listen, Ma, my weed is sitting in the backseat of your car. It's vacuumed sealed so you can't smell it. Go ahead and handle that. When you get the keys, take it in the apartment. I'll meet up with you in a few hours."

"I got you, Daddy," she obliged stepping out the room behind him.

Tipton walked past, Lisa and pulled ten-hundred-dollar bills from his left pocket. "Take care." He placed it in her palm and walked out.

****

Tipton pulled in front of Rex's crib and looked at his cell that read ten-thirty in the morning. The sun was beaming hard, even though it was a Saturday. He still had to be cautious about waking Rex's grandmother. She was old school when it came down to pulling in front of her spot. If you weren't playing Al-Green or church music, your radio was surely gonna be turned off. If you were smoking weed on her back porch, you better had showed up with a carton of those nasty ass Maverick cigarettes she liked to puff on.

Tipton was different if you didn't answer your cell within two calls, he was pulling off because getting out of the car wasn't an option. He dialed Rex's number, then he picked up on the second ring sounding like he'd jumped out the fucking bed.

"Yeah, what up, bruh?"

"I'm outside."

"Smooth, I'll be out in two minutes." Rex hung up.

Keeping his word as always, within a minute and thirty, he was walking out of his front door.

"Nigga, you sound like you jumped out of the bed," Tipton said cranking the car.

"I had to, not answering the phone for you is like Neo missing the payphone call in the matrix. I'll be stuck in the house forever." Rex smiled as they pulled off.

Removing a bundle of money from his pocket, Rex placed it in Tipton's console. "That's three thousand right there, bro."

"Cool, when Peaches finish handling this business for us we can stop by my new spot so I can load you back up."

"Smooth, I guess you finally decided to get the hell on from, Aunt Jemima's spot, huh?"

"Facts, I can't even get pussy in peace," Tipton replied.

"Bruh, you gotta tell me. Does Peaches got that backhand slap you like in Baby Boy pussy? Or is it like that freaky ass sex scene with Jada Pinkett and the bank manager on, Set it off pussy?"

"I'ma have to go with the sex scene from Set it off." Tipton laughed while keeping his eyes on the road.

"Oh, my God! That baby hitting like that?" Rex said with a look as if he was about to cry.

All Tipton could do was flash his pearly whites. "I'm fucking with shorty."

It didn't take long before the fellas were sliding down Dejuan's street. Parts of the Southside was just ratchet. You always had to keep your eyes open because it was no telling what to expect while pushing through Grove Street. Summertime was fastly approaching and the last week of school would begin after the weekend was out. The time to accumulate money the long way was here which meant one thing. Plenty of robbing ass niggas. After honking the horn twice, Rex and Tipton stepped out of the car to smoke the rolled-up joint that rested in the ashtray.

"Oh, shit, guess what Chocolate told me," Rex said nearly choking on the weed.

"What?"

"Remember the night we came through her party?"

"Yeah. What about it?"

"Dejuan said he was in the back smashing, but really he was pulling a Law and Order."

"What the fuck are you talking about, Rex?"

"Chocolate said that crazy ass nigga raped her."

"Get the fuck outta here!"

"That's what I said until she started explaining what happened. It sounded like she was telling the truth."

Running that night back through his head, Tipton remembered Dejuan acting strange when they arrived. Even when it was time to leave, he was sweating like he'd ran a thirty-day marathon. It was also weighing on his mind, why she didn't just call the police?

"That's crazy," was all Tipton could say as they watched Dejuan's mama walk out of the house.

"Tippp, hey, baby boy!"

"How you doing, Ms. Shirley?"

"I'm good. Can you loan mama ten dollars to go and get the laundry cleaned today, boo?"

Without hesitation, Tipton reached in the car and grabbed a fifty-dollar bill. "Here you go, mama."

"Bless yo' heart, baby. My lazy ass son on his way out here," she said with a disgusted look before walking off.

"Why you gotta come out of your pocket when her son getting money now? This ain't Hosea feed the hungry."

"It doesn't matter. She asked me, obviously he ain't doing what he's supposed to do."

After a few minutes passed, Dejuan stepped out of the crib with a heated look on his face. Without speaking, he got in the car and shut the door.

"What bit that nigga in the ass?" Rex laughed, tossing the blunt roach on the ground.

Giving a nonchalant shrug, Tipton jumped in the front seat, starting the car. He looked at his phone, seeing the text from Peaches.

//: We good to go, Daddy.

//: Good job, Ma, I'll be there in a second. Tipton quickly replied and slid off.

"Here go yo' paper, my nigga." Dejuan leaned forward and tossed the roll of money into Tipton's lap. "I gotta straighten you on three hundred."

Hearing the remark, Tipton glared at him through the rearview mirror. His off-balanced posture indicated something was wrong with him. Not to mention coming short on the reup. There was one thing Tip hated and that was to play with his intelligence. He reminded himself to have a personal talk with him later. He wrote the stupid mistake down in his book as strike one.

Chapter 4

The guys sat on the hardwood floor in the living room of Tipton's new townhouse, breaking down the new shipment of marijuana.

"Say, ma, can you step in the other room and call rent-a-center about delivering that tomorrow?" Tipton looked over at Peaches.

After watching her disappear to the stairs, he cut his eyes over at Dejuan. "Say, Juan, wassup with you being three hundred short, bro? I thought we had an agreement on half and half? You get three thousand, I get three," Tipton said with a respectful tone.

Dejuan stopped what he was doing and a mug formed on his face. "Damn, nigga, I gave you twenty-seven hundred. I told you I'ma get the three hundred. Don't be pressing me about that little ass paper."

As he looked from Tipton to Dejuan in silence, Rex knew something was about to escalate.

Tipton's eyes got extremely low as he stood to his feet. This was something you only saw when he was stupid heated. "Let me explain some to you, Dejuan. I cut you in on this before I went outside of the circle to work with any off-brand nigga. I can tolerate a lot, but I refuse to sit back and watch you play with my paper."

"Nigga, fuck that petty ass three hundred dollars. You act like you hurting. Getting all aggressive about that shit."

"Nah, I ain't getting aggressive. But the next time you come out yo' mouth sideways, I won't hesitate to beat yo' ass nigga," Tipton spat stepping in his face.

"Aye look, come on y'all. We got too much going on for y'all to be doing this. We boys man, y'all trippin'." Rex stepped in between them.

"Damn, nigga, you gonna fight me about three hundred bucks? I told you I was gonna straighten that. You said this

money shit wasn't gonna come between us!" Dejuan yelled
with his heart beating fast.

"Like I said, if we getting money, we all gonna come correct, even me. You either, rocking right and eating with us. Or
you can get the fuck on and come up on your paper the hard
way. Ain't no emotions in this shit boy, make yo choice." Tipton slanted his eyes toward him.

"Whatever you say, man," Dejuan replied humbly taking
his seat back on the floor.

"This ain't just my shit. It's all of ours, but what will we
have if I let this shit crumble," Tipton stated before helping
them break down the rest of the weed.

****

After dividing up the twenty pounds of weed, Tipton made
his way to Dejuan's house to drop him off first. Once he pulled
out of the parking lot, he and Rex drove around in silence until
Rex finally spoke up.

"Aye look, man, I know Dejuan blowed you today, but you
already know how that nigga is Tip. He's a fuck-up, but he still
our boy." Rex tried to thin out the animosity between the two.

"Listen, excuses don't care who tell 'em, Rex. They just
wanna be told. I learned everything I know from watching my
mom growing up. No one else, if it wasn't for her, I would be
lost. I make paper to eat and provide for another day. Dejuan
wants a nigga to baby him. If his own mom won't do it, what
makes you think I am?"

"That's true, I think he just got some personal shit buzzing
through his head."

"Well, that's a problem he gotta fix on his own." Tipton
shook his head.

"Do you really think he did that shit to, Chocolate?"

Thinking hard before he answered, Tip looked over at Rex.
"It's only one way to find out."

****

As they listened to Chocolate spill the story, Rex and Tipton could hear the pain in her voice. "Rex, do you mind if I speak to Tip alone for a second?"

"Sure, I'm sorry about what happened to you. Stay up, sis." He headed back for the car.

"Look, Tip, I know Dejuan is your friend and all, but the only reason I didn't get him locked up was because I know you hustle and he's around you all the time."

"I understand, but I can't force you not to say nothing if you telling me what he did is true."

"It is when he grabbed me I told him I didn't wanna get down with him like that. I told him that I liked you and he got even more aggressive and mad."

Tipton stood up and pulled seven grams of purple Kush from his pocket. "Smoke on that by yourself and just relax. I'll slide through tomorrow and shoot you some paper flow for keeping it real like you did," he said before preparing to leave.

"Thanks."

"You good?"

"Tip," she uttered before he could walk off.

"Yeah?"

"You need to watch, Dejuan. That boy envies you. He's not your real friend," Chocolate warned with sincerity in her eyes.

"Say less," he responded before heading back to the car.

"What did she say, bruh, is everything smooth?" Rex sat back with a cool posture.

"She's fucked up off that shit, but she'll be okay. We just gotta focus on getting this money." He frowned keeping her last statement to himself.

"Shit, cheer up then, my nigga. You know I got yo' back like a pimple. Everything gonna be good."

Tipton glared out into the night sky and sighed. "I hope so."

****

Monday Morning

It was a little past 8:30 when Tipton pulled his Dodge Charger into the school's parking lot. He got out and looked up at the cloudy sky before entering the building. As he walked toward the cafeteria, he was stopped.

"Tip, Juan down in the gym getting into it with, Skeet. You might need to get down there now," a young girl yelled out of breath.

Without hesitation, Tip took off full speed cutting through the main lobby, making it out of the door. He shot across to the gym and entered a huge crowd that was huddled together. As he struggled to make his way through the thick group of teens, he witnessed Rex trying to hold Dejuan back. His nose was bleeding profusely and judging from his ripped shirt, Dejaun had gotten his ass beat.

Dejuan was a red nigga standing no bigger than 5'5, his skinny frame and one-hundred-thirty pounds made it hard for him to stand up to anyone.

"What's going on?" Tipton stepped in front of everyone.

"That bitch ass nigga swirled me!" Dejuan shouted trying to break free from Rex's strong grip.

"If it ain't the rich guy. Don't tell me you coming to save this lil weenie?" Skeet laughed along with four niggas, who were posted behind him as if they were straight killers.

Skeet was the true asshole of the school. Most of his time was spent bullying weak links and causing absurd trouble for no apparent reason. His size intimidated most and nothing stopped him from causing havoc inside the walls of West Lake High.

"First, I'ma see what's the problem. Then the rest can be decided after." Tipton looked Skeet in the eyes.

"Ya homeboy needs to learn some manners when he talks to a real street nigga. This ain't elementary school and ain't nothing 'bout me pussy. He stepped on my motherfucking kicks and I told his busta ass to watch where he was walking. The rest was history after he started popping all that gorilla shit."

After looking down at the pair of white Air Force Ones on Skeet's feet, Tipton dug in his pocket and pulled out a large bankroll. "Here's two hundred dollars. You should be able to buy two pairs with that." He held the money out to Skeet.

As he snatched it from Tiptons fingers, Skeet smiled. "See that's very appropriate, right there. At least somebody knows how to compensate a nigga from going through all this hassle. Keep your puppy in control." Skeet then walked off.

"Nigga, fuck you, you better believe this shit ain't over!" Dejuan yelled with venom pumping from his tongue.

After the situation was smoothly handled by Tipton, the crowd slowly dispersed. "Just chill," Tipton said as Dejuan held a shirt up to his nose.

"Chill? Nigga that pussy just swung on me and bust my shit. The only thing that's gonna be chilling is that nigga's body on a slab at the morgue."

"Yeah, and that would've been okay if you wouldn't have let the entire fucking school know. If you do something to him now, everybody is gonna point the finger at you, smart guy."

"The boy Skeet really did too much, Tip. It's like he really wanted to start some shit. I know them niggas with him be toting guns and shit. That's the only reason I didn't kung-fu slap that boy to the floor," Rex lied.

Glancing around for a second, Tipton placed his attention back on them. "Let's get the fuck out of here, I got somebody I want y'all to meet."

After making it out of the gym, they maneuvered to Tip's car and pulled away from the school's ground.

"Where the hell we going?" Rex asked?

"Gwinnett," Tip replied, sliding onto the expressway.

****

After cleaning Dejuan up, the boys arrived at their destination around ten o'clock. The large suburban home was mounded with a black fence and the area was flooded with cars that would require a seventy-thousand-dollar salary to drive off the lot. Tipton's vehicle, on the other hand, looked as if three teenagers was about to commit a burglary.

After exiting the car, they headed up the driveway until they reached the huge front porch. "I hope you, niggas ain't scared of animals," Tipton warned them.

"What the fuck you mean animals? What this nigga got in here, a rhino?" Rex joked.

Before he could reply, the door was unlocked and opened. The appearance of the white man who stood before them seemed like he hadn't slept in weeks. His hair was fuzzy and the AC/DC shirt he wore smelled like a pound of ganja.

"Tip, I thought you weren't stopping by until the moon went to sleep, bro?"

"Change of plans, I need to holla at you about some new business."

"Cool. Who's your friends here? Angry man looks like he's in need of some really good pot." He looked at Dejuan.

"This is Rex and the mean guy is, Juan. Guys this is, Shaggy."

"Nice to meet you, little aliens. You guys feel like blazing some trees or what?" He said before stepping back into the house.

"Hell yeah." Rex moved right behind him.

They entered the crib and Tipton locked the door behind them. The living room alone had Rex and Juan in a trance. All the walls were painted with different graffiti art and there was an extravagant fish tank that stretched around the room. It held over seven baby sharks.

"You guys kick back, roll you a joint or two," Shaggy offered while pulling the tops off the glass containers on his table.

Rex and Juan moved toward the sofa, as Tipton smirked and made themselves comfortable.

"Tip, this man got clear blunt papers. I don't ever wanna go home." Rex smiled and grabbed a bud of exotic.

"Be careful not to drop any of that on the floor. Sizzle will eat that shit, I don't got the energy for the vet, right now."

"Who the fuck is, Sizzle?" Dejuan looked around for a small cat.

"My pet Python, he's sitting under the table," Shaggy said lighting a giant doobie.

Looking down at the gigantic yellow snake, the fear of God moved through his body making him jump up. "Man, what the fuck!" Juan yelled as Tipton burst out into a fit of laughter.

"Shit, I ain't scared of snakes. That bitch gon' have to eat me." Rex shrugged and lit his weed.

"Bruh, this man got a fucking anaconda in his crib, let's go!"

"Chill little angry alien, Sizzle is a vegetarian He don't eat nothing but fruit and hamsters."

"I told you." Tipton motioned for Shaggy to come to the kitchen.

After walking through the dining room, Shaggy led them to the golden stash. Crates were lined against his wall and nearly stacked to the ceiling. All of them were filled with a different flavor of marijuana. "We have white rhino, cranberry kush, tropical fruit, and Skittles. I got moon rocks, Girl Scout cookies, white widow and train wreck. You name it, I got it," Shaggy said pulling on his joint.

"I think I just pissed myself." Rex stared at all the buckets of reefa.

"I'll take my usual twenty supply. You can mix it up for me. I was wondering, what else do you have on the market?" Tipton asked with a finger on his chin.

"I mean sure, I have acid strips. Those little papers are over powerful on the mind man. It'll have you tweaking out a bit." Shaggy waved his hand in a funny motion.

"I'm not into the rave party shit. What else you got?"

"I got some groovy X pills, Zanny bars, and Perkys."

"What the hell are these?" Dejuan touched the tall glass jar that sat on the kitchen table.

"I don't think you want that trip little alien, those are mushrooms."

"I was thinking more on the line of coke," Tipton cut straight to the point.

Smiling, Shaggy took a puff of the rolled backwood. "Miss USA, I'm sorry bro. Me and the white girl don't hang tight anymore."

"I don't understand?"

"Cocaine brings too many problems and bad vibes. I stick to the hippie drugs my friend."

Understanding his reasoning, Tipton pulled two-grand out of his pocket. "How many different pills can I get for this?"

Shaggy thumbed through the cash and smirked. "A bag full little bro. You're like the most awesome little drug lord I know."

After twenty-five minutes of weighing up his package, the boys left with a new product and a giant rolled blunt of blue cheese, handpicked from the tree.

"Shaggy is like the coolest white boy on earth. I think I'm about to change my religion." Rex stopped to light the chronic.

Tipton chuckled. "What you wanna be now, Rex?"

"A hippie! You know what they say. Once you go white, you get high as a kite."

Sharing a laugh, the three of them climbed into the car and headed back to the city.

Chapter 5

Friday

Within a week, things were moving swiftly for the trio. Pills were flying for ten dollars a pop and Shaggy promised to keep Tipton loaded with a thousand plus after he showed back up for more the next week. Teens and even old heads on the street were losing their minds about the new batch. The minority would settle for the lesser, but if you wanted the quality, it was coming from the three hunchos of the block.

After getting dressed for the last day of school, Tipton slapped Peaches across her bare ass. She pulled her attention from the iPad to look up at him.

"How I look, bae?"

His crisp Burberry slacks were tailored to fit him to perfection. The Gucci loafers that rested on his feet complemented the three hundred-dollar Gucci belt around his waist. A fresh white tee gripped his arms and the thick waves in his head spun like he'd brushed them throughout his sleep last night.

"You look like a good ass piece of candy, come here." She said in a sexy tone, biting her lip.

He laughed and tilted his head to the side. "I ain't got time to be playing with you, Peaches. You'll fuck around and make me miss school."

"Boy, bring yo ass here. You ain't finna deny me what's mine."

"You right, I can never deny you. But that don't mean I ain't controlling what time it happens, ma."

He placed a kiss on her juicy full lips, her two bottom golds showed as she mugged him. "I hate yo' ass. God shoulda never gave yo' sexy ass no swag."

"I could've sworn that was the reason you loved me." He smiled as he walked out of the bedroom door. Before she could sling the pillow at him.

Tipton sprinted out of the front door and walked down the driveway, Juan and Rex posted against his car like they were ready for a double XXL interview.

"Goddamn, Rico Suave. You took long enough. I thought you mighta been cutting the slits in ya pants while we been sitting here this entire time," Rex complained.

"Sounds like a hater to me." Tipton climbed in the driver's seat with a smile. Then he looked back at Dejuan whose face was balled up, he placed his attention back to Rex.

"What the hell is wrong with him?"

"Son look like the sour patch man don't he? That nigga tweaking off the new X pills Shaggy gave us. I told him to leave that shit to these folks on the street."

"I think I like him just like that. I'ma start calling you, Grandpa Juan," Tipton said pulling off. Shooting two middle fingers, he placed his dark shades on his face, as they skated toward West Lake High School.

****

School was pumping with the usual paper flow. Everybody wanted to get a taste of the new prescription pills the fellas were dishing out. Certain undercover teachers were placing their orders on the sly and the entire eleventh-grade hallway smelled like a fresh cropped weed farm.

Rex tapped Tipton with his arm, nodding in the direction of Skeet and his crew moving towards them. "Yo' Tip, let me holla at you for a minute, rich man."

Anticipating the bustas were about to make a false move, Juan gripped the pistol handle under his shirt.

Tipton closed the space between them and looked into his eyes. "Waddup?"

"I hear you the man, I need to speak to about getting a bag or two?" Skeet folded his arms.

"Yeah, gram bags. How many you need?"

Skeet laughed and rubbed the bridge of his nose. "I need a pound, my nigga."

"I don't know what you talking about. You might need to go and holla at the dope boys out on Cleveland Ave."

"Damn, my guy, it's like that?"

"That's what it is, my guy."

"Bet, I appreciate ya time, rich guy." Skeet held his palm out to shake Tipton's hand.

Looking down at the cursive L on Skeet's wrist, Tipton's mind flashed to the night his mother was murdered. His words struggled to release as if his soul was snatched from the top of his body. His hands began to shake, as the group departed from his presence.

"Bro, you good?" Rex noticed the bewildered look in his eyes.

"The tattoo," Tipton whispered nearly in tears.

"*Tattoo*, what are you talking about? You sure you ain't pop none of that X?" Rex looked in his low brown eyes.

"The tattoo on his wrist. It's the same tat the nigga had who killed my mom."

"Maybe it's just a coincidence, my nigga. It probably just looks like it's the same," Dejaun said, still gritting his teeth.

"It's the same fucking tattoo! I could never forget no shit like that. It's in the same spot, written in cursive and all," Tipton raged with veins protruding from his neck.

The few teens who stood around paused to see what the loud commotion was about. Rex grabbed Tipton and pulled him over toward the school's bathroom.

"You gotta calm down and think about what you're saying, bro. That nigga ain't nothing but seventeen. If yo' mama died three years ago, that would have made Skeet fourteen. He probably ain't even know how to take the safety off a gun yet."

Even though Rex was making sense, no one could change the feeling Tipton was experiencing in his heart at that time. The dreadful night his queen was taken flipped through his brain like a rerun of a TV show.

"I don't give a fuck if he did it or not. He knows something, I can tell by the way he looked at me. That bitch is about to die, today!" Tipton pushed off and headed to his homeroom class.

Rex looked at Dejuan with a helpless expression, shaking his head. "You heard what bruh said? That nigga gotta go, simple. I want get back for what that bitch boy did to me anyway." Dejuan flashed the handle of his .380 automatic and walked off.

****

3:29 p.m.

Sitting in his seat, Tipton's palms were itching to make it back to his charger when the bell rung. Ms. Berrett eyed him every twenty minutes throughout the day sensing his bad energy. Nothing was gonna get in his way and in his opinion, Skeet had made his own bed. Now he would have to lay in it.

As the bell rang loudly, everyone dispersed from the classroom. "Tipton, can I speak with you please?" Ms. Barrett asked.

Tipton ignored her, continued brushing pass Rex forcefully and pushed through the exit door. He jogged down the flight of stairs, made it to the main floor and exited the school. Light raindrops started drizzling from the sky when he reached his car, he popped the trunk, removed his Glock 17 handgun and placed it on the side of his hip. Within seconds everyone was pouring out of the school signaling that the last day was over.

Dejuan and Rex eased out of the building and proceeded toward the car.

"Tip, look, man, we on school ground. Let's just think about this—"

"Just walk off, Rex. I'm not making you wait around for shit," Tipton cut him off.

Dejaun kept his eyes on all the movement, waiting for the target.

"I'm not walking off nowhere, bro. You my dawg and you trippin'."

"Yo' Tip, there that nigga go," Dejaun said, grabbing his attention.

Tipton spotted Skeet and his entire world froze. His heartbeat sped up, but everything around moved as if it was in slow motion. Skeet noticed the two of them heading directly for him, but he didn't expect the pistol that came from behind Tipton's back.

"Tipton, no!" Ms. Berrett said catching him in the act.

As Skeet tried to make a run for it, hell instantly broke loose. *Boc! Boc! Boc! Boc! Boc! Boc!* The gun erupted violently. Tipton fired his Glock recklessly trying to end the life of his enemy. Screams erupted and teens began to scatter. As Tipton chased Skeet through the main parking lot. Dejuan wasted no time pulling his .380 releasing shots at the rest of his crew. So many people were running in the crowd that he didn't care where the bullets landed.

Firing a lucky shot, Tipton blew a hole through Skeet's leg forcing him to collapse on the ground, panting hard. The light rain began to pour, as he walked closer to him.

"Don't kill me," Skeet mumbled with both hands covering his face.

While listening to his plea, Tipton glanced around at everyone who stood on the sideline, watching in horror. His eyes roamed around until they landed on Ms. Berrett who screamed the word no while shaking her head in tears. Realizing his anger had gone too far, he made a run for his car. Tipton jumped inside and crank the engine just as Dejuan slid into the passenger seat. Then he swerved out of the lot with his tires screeching, Tipton thought about how he'd just flipped the last day of school into a tragedy.

"Why the fuck didn't you kill that nigga, bro? He gonna probably snitch, Tip." Dejuan boosted the situation.

"Just let me think, please stop talking, Juan," Tipton said looking in the rearview. He was doing seventy-five on the dash. "Look, I'm going to drop you off, bro. I don't need you getting caught up with me. Just take some money and lay low for a few days."

"A'ight."

"Do you hear me? I need you to lay low, Juan. No moving period."

"I said I got you, bro. I hear you," Dejuan assured.

Tipton pulled into a nearby gas station and stopped to let him out. After giving him the gun and all the cash in his pocket, he smashed off, heading for his apartment. Hearing his phone ring, he glanced at Rex's name on the screen and shook his head. Tipton answered and placed it to his ear without speaking.

"Don't go home, bro. They already looking for you. The entire school is flooded with cops," Rex said through the receiver.

Letting down the window, Tipton tossed the phone out into the rain. Feeling his mind about to crash, he thought about Peaches. There was nothing he could tell the authorities to get out of the shitty situation he would eventually have to face. All he could do was drive and ponder his next move.

****

Tipton has been sitting at the Oakland City train station for the past four hours, smoking blunt after blunt out of the ounce he stashed in the glove compartment. His mind was so distraught, that he popped two of the Percocet pills to ease his tension. After reiterating the same line in his head over and over again he came to a conclusion that nothing could give him a pass on the charge he was facing. Making the decision to turn himself in, he cranked up his car. The choice he made to shoot Skeet was a choice he definitely was not about run from. In the end, he couldn't blame anyone else for his actions.

After driving for the next thirty minutes, Tipton turned into the parking lot of the townhome complex. The flashing blue lights that surrounded the street caused him to sigh deeply. He put fire to his last blunt, the thought of running was out of the question. He pulled down toward the house and got out with a drunken stagger.

"Mr. White put your hands on top of your head and get on the ground," A black crime scene officer ordered with a firm voice. His hands were gripping on a black pistol.

While still inhaling on the blunt, Tipton did as he was told. Two officers walked slowly over to him with precaution, restrained him and placed cuffs on his wrist. Then they stood him to his feet and the black detective snatched the blunt from his mouth before shaking his head.

"That's my boyfriend, I got the right to speak with him. Get the hell off him!" Peaches screamed moving over to them. "Tip, what did you do, baby?"

Feeling subdued by the pills, all he could do was lean. "I'm—" He paused and placed a kiss on her lips. "Get me a lawyer, ma. Everything is gonna be okay."

"Tipton White, you're under arrest for aggravated assault on the victim at West Lake High School. You have the right to remain silent, anything you say can and will be used against you in the court of law. You have the right to an attorney. If you can't afford one, one will be appointed to you. Would you like to talk about this matter?" The detective questioned after reading him his Miranda rights.

"Can I smoke my last blunt before you take me to jail?"

"Take him away."

They escorted him to the police cruiser, put him in the backseat and headed for the county jail for booking.

Chris Green

Chapter 6
Gwinnett County Jail
Two weeks later

"Why in the fuck is these people housing you here? I thought you were supposed to be at Fulton?" Rex spoke through the visitation phone.

"They told me it was overcrowded. These have been the hardest few days of my life. I hate this shit. They told me I was being charged as an adult when I'm only sixteen," Tipton stressed with a hand on his forehead.

"I told you, bro. This is what I was trying to warn you about. You too smart for that dumb ass shit you pulled."

"I know, my lawyer said they offering me five years on a plea. I think I'm just gonna ride with the five."

"What the hell we supposed to do without you for that long?" Rex mouthed feeling there had to be a different option.

"The exact same thing, I'm leaving you in charge of my shit, bro. I'm putting my faith in you because no one else is fit to handle it, but you."

"I don't think I'm ready for no shit like that, Tip. I—"

"You are ready. Just because I'm not gonna be there for a little while doesn't mean the show has to slow down. If you stop, then everything else stops. We have a foundation, I need you to enforce it even harder. I'm gonna leave you the connect and you have access to my paper. So, you don't have to go through the hassle with anyone. All you gotta do is get that money. I need something to come home to," Tipton said with inspiration in his tone.

"That's word on my life, bro. I got you no matter what." Rex bumped his fist against the glass.

"Fucking right, let me scream at Peaches before my time is up."

"Bet, hold it down, my nigga. Keep a death grip on that soap." Rex smiled before handing his girl phone.

Tipton laughed to himself, then stared at Peaches' beautiful face as she sat in the seat. Even through the glass, his attraction and love grew for her every minute he sat behind the wall.

"I miss you." She stared off with a sad expression.

"No frowns we too busy being happy, Peaches. You know, I love you."

"I'm pregnant with your child and you about to go to prison. It's hard not to frown, Tip."

"And just like I told you, everything is gonna be okay. I want you at every visit with my little one. I'm gonna head down here and get all the things done that I need to get out sooner. Since I met you, I said hard times that relationships have will separate the weak from the strong. All we got is each other."

"I'm not leaving your side. People can talk and say what they want, but my position is where I stand firmly. My pussy is aching so bad for you." She grinned.

"Oh yeah?"

"Yep." She flashed him one of her gorgeous breasts.

"You gon' make me get kicked out of this visitation for stripping butt naked on yo' ass." He smiled.

"Well, that's gonna make two of us cause I'ma bounce this ass all in front of the glass for my daddy."

"We gon' hold off on all that until I can touch you. I promise that all is gonna be okay, though. My baby is gonna be spoiled at any cost and my love will always run deep for you," he assured.

"I know and please don't think you about to be down there all in them little prison bitches face because I will show up to a visit on the bullshit."

"Yo', what are you talking about?" Tipton laughed.

"I'm not playing, Tipton. Those hoes down there be trying to give up pussy and all. Don't make me cut yo' dick off and eat it, nigga," she threatened with slanted eyes.

"Relax, bae, nobody is worried about making no groupie friends. I'm only doing my time so I can get back home."

"White, your visit is over!" The C.O said through the intercom.

Throwing up his thumb, he turned his attention back to Peaches. "Listen, it's time for me to go. I need you to keep a leveled head out there and remember we have an objective to accomplish. It's easy to say something and get sidetracked on your words."

"Tip, stop throwing indirect quotes at me. I'm not gonna jump ship or whatever you feel. I'm grown and if I didn't want to be here, I wouldn't waste your time."

Tipton blew her a kiss through the glass, hung up the phone and headed back to his cell. Regardless of the critical position he was in, family would always be the ones he could count on, or so he thought.

****

Four Years Later

Tipton flicked through his large photo album, staring at his beautiful little daughter. Everything about her reminded him of his mother. Her red rosy cheeks, the long curly hair that laid down her back and the same caramel complexion. The only similarity she shared with Tipton was his low brown eyes. It was an amazing thing to him, seeing a child you birthed grow to be exactly like you. It made him proud to be a father. Unfortunately, after four long years of riding in a prison cell, Peaches decided to go out and get some taste of a lil' dick that eventually flipped her completely off the boat. Things were perfect during the beginning of his bid she never missed a visit. Her love and words seemed so sincere and genuine, but all the good game she spilled finally dried up like a rotten prune. Phone calls started to go unanswered. Money started to be misplaced and the streets started to call her name.

Tipton closed the book and stood up looking in his six-inch mirror. The young mustache he once wore was now connected with a full beard. His medium frame upgraded to a full machine. He'd spent most of his time working out and playing basketball. Being in prison taught Tipton numerous important things that he would never forget. Rule number one, never trust a female's word that she's gonna ride for your bid unless the bitch break in the prison and stay with you until your release date. Rule number two, always read to open your mind up to different things. Nothing was off-limits when it came down to a black man succeeding. It took self-motivation first in order to see progress. Rule number three, never stress no matter how bad things looked. A better day would surely show.

"Yooo' Tipp!" He heard someone scream his name from the dayroom area.

He looked outside his cell door and stared down at his homie, Halo who waved for him to come down. Moving swiftly to his room, Tip stepped in.

"Waddup, my guy?"

"Rex wants you on the phone, God," he replied while brushing his hair.

Halo was a nigga's worst nightmare. Standing six-feet-even with bright red skin, tattoos covered his chest and back. His hand game was extremely lethal, and the authorities would have to come save you if he got ahold of a knife. The scariest thing about Halo was his bright blue eyes. He wasn't mixed or born in a foreign country. He was from a small county out of Omaha, Nebraska. Halo came to Georgia at the age of fifteen to stay with his grandmother. After catching seven years for a manslaughter charge, he was serving his last year along with Tipton.

"My boy, tell me something good," Tipton said after picking up the phone off the bed.

"The same as usual, nigga. Stacking this paper and getting mo' ass than a toilet." Rex laughed.

"Ain't nothing wrong with that. What's been good on them streets lately?"

"The same shit, my guy. Of course, ya brother Dejuan extra flashy out this bitch. He running his mouth telling everybody you about to touch down. It's a lot of new competition out there, but we eating regardless. I saw Peaches when I picked up, Kimmi. She was sitting out the front arguing with some nigga on some pathetic shit."

"Fuck that bitch, I just want my daughter when I get home and it's back to the trio gang," Tipton fumed hearing her name.

"Facts. Oh, I forgot, I been running into this nigga Skeet too."

"Waddup with that busta?"

"He still talking greasy like he wants smoke for that shit. I guess the nigga nuts got big since he and the little crew he been rocking with selling a little weight. Some shit called Louie Gang."

"I been hearing that shit ringing bells in prison. It don't excite me at all. I got big plans for us when I touch bro and it won't be moving weed, I bet ya that."

"Come on, my guy. We don't have to speak on that. I'm pushing the same whip you in no matter what. The hard part is over with," Rex agreed.

"Keep things in order, bro. In due time, the whole city will belong to us."

"With ease, I tossed like two stacks on yo' books, my nigga. That should last you cause I ain't digging in yo' stash no more for shit. You strapped like a shitty diaper boy."

"You stupid." Tipton smiled. "Stay up and out of the way, bro. Tell Dejuan I said calm the fuck down, too."

"Bet, I'll scream at you later fool."

"You already know."

"Smooth," Rex replied before hanging up.

"Why the hell you grinning so hard for, God?" Halo leaned against the wall munching on a bag of chips.

"Because shit is looking lovely for a nigga. Where you thinking about going when you touch down?" Tipton said changing the subject.

Halo shrugged and sat down on his bed. "I don't know, I really ain't got nowhere to go. I might just hit the shelter until I find a job."

Tipton balled up his face and folded his arms. "Nigga you got me fucked up. You can come with me. I got my own shit already. I'm caked up with the dough. You ain't gotta worry about shit. You jumping in my loop and I'm gonna help you get this paper. We like family, bro."

"Blessings God, you know I'm rocking with you at any cost."

"What you good at? You sell weed—dope?"

Halo shook his head, finishing the last of his chips. "Murder," he replied with a straight face.

****

Two Days Later

Rex pulled his white BMW 650 in front of Peaches', parked and jumped out of his whip. He checked the time on his Paul Newman Rolex as he headed up the driveway. He paused and looked over at Dejuan's Lexus sitting on the side of her home. Sparking his blunt, he scratched his head in confusion and continued to the front door. He knocked sternly, then stepped back.

"Who is it?" Peaches yelled from the other side.

"Rex."

Peached detached the locks and opened the door. Her hands were still adjusting her robe. "Kimmi, your uncle here!" he yelled with an aggravated expression.

"What's Dejuan's car doing over here?" he questioned immediately.

"He came and dropped it off a few hours ago. He said he needed somewhere to park it while he went to handle some business, I guess," she lied.

Watching Tipton's daughter appear from behind her, he paused the conversation and smiled. "Wassup, Stinky Butt, you ready to go have some fun?"

Cheesing with that precious grin, Kimmi nodded and jumped into his arms. Ever since Tipton went to prison and Peaches dropped his child, Rex made it his business to go pick her up once a week and splurge on whatever she wanted. It was nothing like a child being away from her father for years at a time. So, building a bond with her was on the strength of Tip being on lockdown.

"Are you good?" he mumbled at Peaches with a disturbed face.

"Go ahead and get in your car seat, Kimmi." Peaches ordered before taking a step further out of the door.

Rex sat her down, then turned around to face her.

"Listen, Rex, I know you Tip's boy or whatever, but you just can't come over here to my shit like you checking me. I don't owe you or him nothing."

"That's where you're wrong, Tipton showed you, mad love. He left you over a hundred grand and you ain't got nothing to show for it. You left him in a chain gang on stick because you weren't woman enough to stick to your word, Peaches."

"Nigga, do you hear how you sound? He left me with a baby. I got rent, bills, a car note, and a mortgage. How long you think those lil' ass stacks gon' last me?"

"Maybe you should've got up and got a job. I watched you spend up my brother's money like you hit the fucking lotto shawty. Regardless of him going to prison, you were way older which means you should have stepped up and got on your grown woman shit. My advice to you, tighten up because bruh on the way home real soon." Rex shook his head.

"Nigga fuck, Tip! I don't need him. Just because y'all lames running around making money for him don't mean I'ma kiss his ass, too. You ain't my man and you ain't eating my pussy. So, you damn sho' don't need to be telling me what I should be doing. All you're here for is to pick up his daughter. Besides that, stay the fuck out of my business," she spat slamming her door.

As he listened to her disrespectful words, Rex could tell she was involved in some other shit. She never had a reason for her lack of loyalty because Tipton made sure she was straight. The closer it got to him coming home, the more hatred grew inside her heart. Logging the slick remark down in his head, Rex made sure to keep a close eye out on her movements.

He headed back to the car with his niece, then dialed Dejuan's number on his cellphone before climbing in, catching the voicemail, he smirked before pulling off. Something seemed very strange with Peaches and before it was all said and done, he was gonna be sure to expose it all.

****

Gwinnett County

"God, can you please give me the strength to get past the little man inside the tree. Gosh!" Shaggy shouted with a blunt in his mouth, as he played the *Call of Duty* modern warfare on his Xbox.

Shaggy heard the doorbell ring, then got up and headed for the door with his eyes still glued on the screen. When he opened the door, the barrel of an Ak-47 assault rifle was shoved into his face.

"Don't open ya mouth or say nothing. Or I'ma split yo' shit like a cabbage cracker," The masked robber ordered with authority.

Shaggy feeling his knees buckle dropped the controller and held his hands high in the air. The cold steel pressed against his nose forced his stomach to grumble in fear before releasing a slight wind of gas.

"First, I wanna know where the money at? Then I want every drug you toting in this motherfucker. And I mean pronto!"

"Listen, bro, I have everything you need just don't waste me, man," Shaggy stated while backing up to the kitchen.

The masked man slammed the butt of his choppa across Shaggy's mouth. Shaggy fell to the floor with massive stars clouding his vision. "I said don't speak! All you need to be doing is grabbing and bagging bitch!" The robber informed with a roll of garbage bags.

Shaggy spit out three of his teeth, as he stood to his feet and walked into the kitchen. He opened the cabinets, grabbed the seven boxes of potatoes and dumped the cash out on the counter.

"That's what I'm talking about, handle that." He opened the bag for Shaggy.

After sacking up the loot, he snatched it from his hands and pointed at the buckets of marijuana. Not wanting to feel another whack from the pistol, Shaggy did what he was instructed to do. He grabbed the crates of weed one by one, quickly filling three trash bags. After the job was complete, he stood still and placed his hands back in the air.

"Is there anything else in the spot I need to know about before I search his bitch? Now is the time to speak."

"All I have is a weed plant and my cellphone dude. It's in the room. You might not wanna go in there, man. My pet, Sizzle is in there."

Smirking, the robber raised his gun and released three lethal shots to Shaggy's chest. *Bak! Bak! Bak!*

After watching him fall over into the pile of crates, the robber stood over him placing another shot to his forehead. Then walked to the bedroom, he stepped past the snake and grabbed the phone off the bed. He sent out a quick text and tossed the phone back on the mattress. He headed back for the kitchen and picked up the jackpot off the floor. Making his way out of the house, he placed it inside the trunk. Then hopped back in the car and glanced in the mirror checking on the little one before slowly pulling off.

Chris Green

Chapter 7

9:00p.m

As he pulled back up to Peaches' crib, Dejuan cursed himself for not waiting after he spotted Rex leaning on his BMW. His arms was crossed and the handle of his pistol was visible. His posture changed when the car came to a halt and the expression he wore on his face wasn't pleasant. Dejuan stepped out of his rental, lit a Newport and closed the distance between them. "Why you standing out here looking like you about to catch a body, my brother?"

"Shaggy's dead," Rex said, staring at him with a stern face.

"That's fucked up. What happened to him?" Dejuan took another pull of his nicotine.

"He was robbed, that shit is all over the news. Any reason you driving around in a rental when you got a sixty thousand dollar car of your own?" Rex asked.

"Nigga, what the fuck is this twenty-one questions? I'm tired of whipping in the same shit, so I went and copped a rental for a few days," Dejuan said with a wrinkled face.

"But why is it parked at Peaches' spot?"

Smirking with an indication of guilt, he laughed. "What you think I'm fucking that bitch or something?"

"You said it, not me," Rex shot back. "It's kinda funny yo' whip parked at our partna's baby mama crib while you riding around in this rental handling business. I tried to hit you up today and couldn't get an answer. Now our plug is mysteriously robbed and killed."

Dejuan pulled on the cigarette forcefully, then slammed it on the ground. "I know you ain't trying to blame me for taking that pussy motherfucker out?"

"It looks like you keep blaming yourself. And yeah, I got a feeling you pulled some bullshit because I know you better than anyone. The same way I know you're fucking, Peaches." Rex rose up off the car.

"Nigga, fuck you, you don't know shit. Ever since that boy, Tip left you in charge of his little operation you got the big head. Nah, I ain't fuck that bitch, but she did suck my dick. And I ain't take Shaggy out either, but I damn sho' thought about it. Does that make you feel better, my nigga?" Dejuan was shouting loud enough to make the neighbor's dog bark.

Rex rubbed a hand through his dreads, as he thought about putting a bullet in his skull just for the disrespect, but he held his composure. "You a real foul nigga for sliding around on Tip's baby mama while he's locked down. After all the love bro showed both of y'all. You spit right back in my guy's face like his loyalty ain't worth shit."

"What? I'm the same nigga that's been out here getting to the paper for this man. Helping this nigga stack his shit to the roof while he caged up and shit! I can't help if that nigga baby mama a freak and I can't change the fact that I'm a street nigga. We don't cuff freaks, we fuck them and split remember," he stated with arrogance.

Rex shook his head in disbelief, eyeing him with hatred. "Make sure you be the first one to keep it real with him when he touches down, Mr. Real Nigga," he spat before getting in his car to leave.

"Dick riding muthafucka!" Dejuan mumbled as he watched his car speed down the street. In his mind, he didn't give a fuck about emotions. Either a nigga would have to respect it or check it.

****

As he worked out in his cell, Tipton was almost at his thousand push up limit. His anger was pumping from the disturbing news that was delivered to Halo's phone. Shaggy wasn't just a plug he was a true friend which made things more personal. There was only a select few that knew the whereabouts of Shaggy's location. Of course, he blamed himself for not being there to handle business instead of sending others. Rex knew

Tipton was going through a lot, so he never mentioned the story regarding Dejaun and Peaches. He decided to let the cards play out until his boy was set free from the slave house.

Tipton stood to his feet and wiped the sweat from his muscular body. The light knock at his door caused his eyes to shift.

"Got any time for an old man to talk to you?" Mr. Bishop stepped in.

"Always, come catch a seat." Tipton tossed on a shirt.

Mr. Bishop sat down at the end of his bed, smiling. "I heard the good news about the parole letter. What plans you got when you touch the streets?"

Mr. Bishop was currently serving a light bid for some miscellaneous charges. As he would always say, no one would ever be perfect. His wise words never fell on deaf ears when he spoke to the dorm. He was highly respected when it came to delivering the message for a brother changing. A black brother at that. He always told Tipton there was a lot of traits in him which he saw in himself. It was his dying mission to give him the game to delete the slips from his future.

"I got a few ideas, I gotta make sure I dodge all the slime shit before I establish anything. It's different out there now, Bishop."

Bishop shook his and leaned forward. "Now you gotta ask yourself when you speak. Do you truly know where slime people come from?" Pondering on the question, Tipton continued to listen. "I'll answer it for you. They come from opening doors to them being your friends. See in order to cause betrayal, one has to let another in enough to see, hear and observe what has you comfortable. The next stage moves one to know if it's worth taking. They try what I call a test run. They lay and pick to see how long you will give until it sucks you dry and leave you with nothing. When you do get to the point where you're eventually tired of giving, it gives them the thought to do what's been eating at them so long, *cross you.*"

As Tipton soaked up every word that slid through his ears, he knew that indulging with too many people is what leaves a man vulnerable.

"How long do you have left now?" Bishop asked.

"Parole said they should be kicking me loose within the next thirty days. None of my people really know besides my uncle."

"Keep it that way. A surprise is better than anything. Creep around for a minute and see who actually missed you. Or who paid for you to stay in."

Tipton shook Bishop's hand and he wasted no time peeling out. Tipton knew a lot of people were expecting the same sixteen-year-old that left the streets forty-eight months ago. What they didn't know was that his mind grew very quickly while he was incarcerated. After he stepped one foot back out on God's earth, only two things would matter. His daughter and the almighty dollar.

Chapter 8

The next thirty days seemed to go by like clockwork, Tipton was sitting in his room laying across the bed when the officer came to his door at seven-thirty in the morning. "White pack your shit, you're out of here."

That statement caused his heart to jump in excitement. It never mattered how hard a nigga was behind the wall. The feeling of being released would have you ready to drop tears. He started throwing miscellaneous items from his steel locker box on the bed.

Halo stepped in the doorway with a huge smile. "It's about that time huh, God?"

Tipton grinned and embraced him with a firm hug. "It's time, Bro. I should be up here bright and early to pick you up from the parking lot."

Working ahead of time, Tipton paid for Halo, one of the best parole lawyers in Georgia. Being that he had under eleven months left, the representative guaranteed him a release the day after him for the fifteen thousand he was compensated.

Halo nodded with gratefulness in his eyes and helped Tipton carry his things to the front. After passing out his commissary and Jordan sneakers, Tip gave Halo the number to call when he was released. He stepped out of the dorm's main door then walked away without looking back.

"I guess you're one of the lucky ones, White? I don't see too many young ones like yourself make it out of here," the officer stated while popping the entrance to main control.

"What you mean by that?" Tipton responded.

"I've been working here for ten years. Most men I see step through that door with a light bid leaves back out in two ways. Catching a life sentence from harming someone else or they prey on the wrong person and leave out in a box, heading to piss ant hill. I've always seen different in you. Take this chance and make it your advantage," he encouraged before releasing the handcuffs.

The officer gave him a pair of beige state pants and a tee shirt to dress out. Tipton signed a document for his check and walked out of the prison door. He closed his eyes inhaling deeply as the sun nibbled on his skin. He felt his entire spirit was clean, and he was reborn.

"It took you long enough," Tip heard a voice speak out to him.

Looking to the right of him, he laid eyes on his Uncle Jackson. He was leaned up against a blue Porsche 718 Boxter S. He was rocking a bald head as usual. His wrist sported a submariner Rolex watch and his apparel was Gucci from head to toe.

"I can decide how fast I move now that I'm on my own time. Waddup, Unc?" Tipton smiled hugging his family.

"You, I guess I can't call you young no more? You bigger than me. Did you learn anything?" He gave a curious look.

Nodding his head, Tipton glanced up at the sun. "Yeah, I learned that time is valuable."

"Exactly." He tossed on his Cartier frames and tapped his shoulder. "Let's take a ride, nephew. You ever drove one of these?"

Staring at the Porsche, Tipton shook his head. "Nah, but it would be nice."

Jackson handed him the keys and climbed in the passenger seat. After sitting behind the wheel, Tipton started the engine. He listened to the lethal motor come to life, then pulled out of the gated prison. Tip took a deep breath and applied some pressure to the gas pedal.

"Tell me something, youngsta. What's ya plan now that you're free?"

"I just wanna live, unc. Make my money quietly as possible and stay out of the way. Everything else is just a waste of energy."

Jackson rolled down his window and lit up his Maduro cigar. "Understood. A man with no plan is guaranteed to fail. So, it's nothing wrong with you feeling that way. I pulled a seven-year bid when you were firstborn. I lost everything from the hands of the system. When I touched back down your mama gave me my jump and I never looked back."

"That's real."

"I hear that you got a mean operation with the weed. You jumping back in or what?"

Thinking about his answer, Tipton shook his head no. "I got bigger bills to pay."

Knowing exactly what he meant, Jackson leaned back in the seat. "It's only right, baby boy. Somebody gotta pick up where yo' mama left off."

After driving for the next thirty minutes, Tipton pulled up to Jackson's five-bedroom home. The brick house sat on six acres of land and a large pond rested in the back yard.

"Welcome home, nephew, come on in."

Both men stepped out of the truck and headed across the driveway to the front door. As they entered the expensive crib, Tipton stared around the luxury living room. Grey suede couches aligned the walls, matching the huge Italian fur rugs that stretched across the entire floor. A sixty-inch, curved flatscreen TV was mounted over a large glass patio door that led to the back yard. Every corner was laced with a unique painting that represented the black struggle of freedom and poverty.

Jackson made his way into the kitchen and grabbed a bottle of silver 1800 along with two small glasses. He poured them both a drink, they toasted to Tipton's release and tossed the shots back. Tipton balled up his face from the taste, denying the next when Jackson offered another.

"Everything you need is upstairs in the front room to the left, clothes and money. Get yourself together, I'll be back in about two hours." Jackson grabbed another drink before heading to the front door.

"I don't need two hours to get dressed. It shouldn't take that long."

Jackson smirked and sipped his cup. "Trust me, you gonna need two hours, maybe more," he replied before leaving out.

Tipton stood to his feet, smiling, as he glanced out at the huge backyard. Now that he was home, he knew it was only a matter of time before he was sitting in his own crib similar to his uncle's. After viewing a little more of the house, he headed upstairs to his room. Upon opening the door, Tipton scratched his chin seeing the two black goddesses stretched out on his bed. Now he was sure, Jackson was right about those two hours.

"Damn, so, you're our treat for this afternoon, huh?" A tan-skinned woman stepped towards him. Her hair was curly, and her face reminded him of Stacy Dash.

"You tell me?" Tipton scanned her phenomenal body up and down.

She pulled him to the bed, then they both crawled to their knees and unbuckled his khaki pants. One eased down his boxers, as the other smiled with satisfaction. The dark-headed woman stood five-two with a slim build. Her almond-shaped eyes glistened with every blink and her hands scanned his body like a professional. The other light-skinned woman was built a little healthier. Her backside was soft, and her skin glowed to perfection. Jet black hair laid neatly down to her shoulders and the red freckles on her face brightened the attraction even more.

It felt wonderful to have two women on the first day of freedom. It was surely a day he wouldn't forget. After taking his time with the girls for the next hour, Tipton finally caught his orgasm and headed for the shower. Before he could place the soap on his body, the girls were stepping in behind him, smiling. They both prepared to wash him before another game of tongue action.

****

After getting out of the shower, Tipton snatched the digits from the two fine sistas before they departed from Jackson's home. It was very pleasing to him with the small-time they shared together, and it definitely wouldn't be the last.

He opened the huge walk-in closet, scanned all the attire and began searching for something to dress himself in. He took down a pair of fitted bleach *Balmain* jeans, grabbed the matching shirt and placed it on his body. The variety of shoes underneath the clothes were easy to decide from when he laid eyes on a pair of white *Balenciagas*. Inspecting himself in the mirror, it was finally official that he was back. He looked at the light brown jewelry box sitting on top of the dresser, opened it up and stared at the Gravity Frank Muller watch.

"Damn!" Tipton said sliding it on his wrist admiring the timepiece.

Spotting the small key that rested inside, he picked it up and smiled. He moved back to the closet and slid the clothes to the side exposing the medium size safe. Using the key, Tipton unlocked it and glanced inside at the stacks of money. A yellow sticky note was attached to a bundle of bills that read: *A hundred for every year plus one more for good luck.*

Tipton placed a nice lump sum in his pockets, closed the safe and headed downstairs. After kicking back in front of the entertainment system for a few minutes, Jackson walked through the door.

"Nephew, I take it you was able to settle in well? You looking real relaxed and rested." He tapped Tipton's shoulder before sitting down.

"That was quite a surprise. I don't think it can get more relaxed than that."

Jackson tossed him a set of keys and looked at his watch. "Welcome back to the world, baby boy. You deserve it. I know you got things you wanna do and people you need to see. I'll meet up with you tomorrow so we can discuss some more business. I'm about to head home and retire."

Staring at him with a confused face, Tipton chuckled. "What do you mean head home. How many spots you got?"

"I never told you this was my house. You're the one holding the keys to this bitch. You can thank your mama for that."

Looking at the car key ring, Tipton stood up. "So, what's this other key for?"

"Check in the garage, it should be something out there for you," Jackson said then walked out the front door.

Trailing out to the garage, Tipton spotted the black *McLaren 720S*. Jackson shot a thumbs up with a nod. Tipton-climed inside and crunk the engine allowing the pressure to release from the pipes. There was nothing that could change the feeling of dropping the top in yo' own foreign. Not to mention the first day free. He slid out of his garage, prepared to reclaim his city.

****

Rex sat in the living room of his three-bedroom home, counted the daily earnings he'd recently picked up from his worker a few hours prior. As he dumped the ashes from his blunt, his cellphone vibrated in his pocket. He pulled it out, looked at the mysterious number and answered.

"Waddup, who dis?"

"Nigga, I been watching you for the past ten minutes. And you still sitting at the table?"

"Tip, boy what kind of freaky shit you got going on? You got a camera in my spot or somethin'?" Rex continued his count.

"Nigga, turn around."

Rotating in his chair, Rex spotted Tipton through the huge glass window. He was leaning against his whip flicking a bird.

"Motherfucker!"

Rex ran out of the crib and picked Tipton off his feet. "They freed, my dawg. Nigga, I should choke yo' ass out like a worthless stripper. Why you ain't tell me nothing? I could've come and got you."

"I was trying to surprise everybody fool. Not only that, my Uncle Jackson, came and picked me up. He dropped a major blessing on me." Tipton nodded towards the car.

"I see you, I gotta take some pictures inside this bitch later on. Come on in." He moved back to the crib.

As he stepped through the threshold, Tipton nodded in approval. "Nigga, yo' shit look like a female decorated this bitch."

"Come on, man. You know my granny came over here with that old 1926 decoration shit. I called extreme home makeover the day she left."

Laughing, Tipton took a seat at the kitchen table. "So, wassup, my guy? What's been going on for the past few weeks?"

Grabbing a fresh Cigarillo off the refrigerator, Rex caught a seat and started to bust down for a roll-up session. "Money has been flowing smooth, bro. I got a few workers moving the bags for us out on the Westside. Them young niggas hungry and they legit. I started playing around with a little bit of the pills again. Shit hasn't really been right with that ever since we lost, Shaggy."

"So, you found another weed plug?"

"Yep, he got the bags for the cheap, too. Area pressure, you know I'm taking advantage of that. I got about a hundred and fifty put up for you, too. Whenever you ready for it, I can grab it."

"That's love. Waddup with, Dejuan?"

Rex lit the blunt and shook his head. "That nigga just crazy, man. He don't give a fuck about nobody but himself. I'm throwing you a welcome home party tomorrow night at club Mansion. He will come through when he knows you're out."

"That's cool." Tipton accepted the weed. "After we see what that nigga talking about then I can lay the plan down on you about what I'm trying to do. We can still make a few plays off the weed, but we ain't gonna touch it ourselves. I'm 'bout to get this kitchen opened, so we can bring in this real chedda. It's no point taking prison chances out here petty hustling."

"You home now, my guy. Whatever move you make, I'm with you. Just be ready for this party tomorrow, nigga." Rex bumped fists with his friend.

"Facts, I'm about to snatch up Kimmi and get a little daddy and daughter time. Hit my phone and keep me posted." Tipton headed for the door.

"Will do! Say, fool?" Rex stopped him.

"Waddup?"

"Welcome home, bro."

"Don't cry on me. We ain't even had no fun yet," Tip said before walking out.

Rex chuckled, tapping his finger on the table before he started back counting his paper. Seeing Tipton's face, made him realize a lot of things were about to change in the city of Atlanta.

Chapter 9

Tipton arrived at Peaches' small two-bedroom home and stepped out of his whip, heading through the grass up to the front door. He knocked and waited patiently for an answer. He heard movement on the other side, then Peaches opened the door.

She froze with a stunned expression on her face as she stared into his eyes. "Tip?" She stepped toward him.

"Hey, Peaches," he replied in a dry tone.

She jumped into his arms and latched around his neck and waist, planting sweet kisses to his face and cheeks. "I can't believe you're really here," she whined with fake tears.

Tipton placed her back on the ground and stepped back from her. "Where's my daughter?"

The crudeness and immaturity Peaches showed while Tipton was incarcerated had turned his heart cold. His devotion to her was a hundred percent genuine and she still showed her true colors by turning her back at the worst time of his life. It was something he couldn't forgive, or forget.

"Oh, I guess you too good for a bitch now, huh?" Peaches spat with a hand on her hip.

Even after four years, her body was still amazing. Her beautiful face and skin still glowed, but her devilish aura had increased remarkably. Tipton could feel it pumping through her veins.

"I just came for, Kimmi."

"But I asked you a question, nigga! I'm yo' baby mama and you standing in front of me like you ain't miss this. You must don't want pussy no mo'?"

As he shook his head, Tipton's anger began to rise. "Check this, you left me down bad in prison behind a wall. After all the love I showed you. Making promises you couldn't keep was foul, but I respect it. I have no ill feelings against you shawty, I just want my baby."

"Nigga you ain't dicked this pussy down or gave me no kiss. You ain't even told me you love me, but you think you finna take my baby and get the fuck on. Bitch, you might as well get back in your car and pull off." Peaches got in his face.

He grabbed her by the throat forcefully and kissed her lips aggressively. Then shoved a hand inside her thin shorts, clawing his nails into her ass. "This what you want, bitch?"

"That's right, Daddy. Show me I'm still yo' bitch," she cried with a psycho expression while he continued to choke her.

He knew at that point Peaches was a complete lunatic. He pushed her out of his personal space, she stumbled backward. Before she could swing back, Kimmi popped inside of the doorway.

"Dadddyyy!" she yelled with excitement, leaping in his arms.

Tipton held her close while giving Peaches the look of death. He walked off to the car, strapped her in the backseat and got in to leave.

****

After spending hours having fun with his little one, Tipton glanced in the mirror observing his princess in a light sleep. A round of Monkey Joes and a five-thousand-dollar shopping spree had his little mini-me tired. The time he spent with Kimmi felt so great, he never wanted it to end. He snatched him up a small bottle of Henny and drove around I-285 four more times. No matter how bad he wanted shit to be perfect, things were at a critical standpoint. His heart wanted his family together but falling for lies and betrayal was like a Ferris wheel. It was a circle of life that was bound to come back around and show you the same face again.

Realizing it was getting late, Tipton jumped off the interstate and headed back to Peaches' crib. He pulled in front of the door, grabbed his baby out of the backseat and headed inside.

He walked inside without knocking and placed her on the living room couch next to Peaches.

"You could've alerted me that you were on the way back. My number is still the same, Tip."

"Too late, I'm already here."

He kissed his baby forehead, then headed outside to grab the things he purchased for her.

"Baby, I need to talk to you." Peaches stepped in front of him before he could leave.

"Peaches, just leave me alone. I just wanna go home," his speech was slurred.

"Just come in the room so I can speak to you without waking our baby. After we talk you can leave." Peaches held onto his shirt so he couldn't move.

Obeying her pleas, Peaches led him to the bedroom and locked the door behind her. She dropped her robe to the floor, her seductive body glowed as if she'd just bathed in a tub of warm baby oil.

"I didn't come here for this," Tipton mumbled when she pushed him back on the bed.

"I don't give a fuck. You gon' let me please this dick tonight, nigga." Peaches got on her knees, forcing his rod through the zipper of his jeans.

Her eyes widened with delight at his growth. She smiled and quickly downed him in her warm throat. As she squeezed his manhood, Tipton turned his head to block her face from his sight. She arched her ass, slurped and spit on it numerous times to excite herself more. Knowing he couldn't resist her sex game Tipton leaned back on the bed and grabbed the back of her head. Her eyes began to tear up when he forced himself deeper into her mouth and snatched her head lightly. Peaches caught a deep breath and jumped back to work. Using two hands, she massaged his shaft in a circular motion while sucking on his head like a baby bottle.

"Bust in my mouth, Daddy," she moaned while using her long tongue to tease him.

Ignoring her, Tipton stood up and dropped his jeans. He snatched her off the floor, placed her on the bed and arched her ass to face him. Then grabbed her by the hair with a firm grip and plunged his monstrous manhood into her slippery slit.

"Ahh shit!" She grabbed the sheets, feeling explicit pleasure.

He slammed a hard hand down on her round ass and pumped harder between her soft cheeks. Feeling her first orgasm erupt, Peaches' eyes began to roll in satisfaction.

Tipton couldn't control himself. The liquor was kicking in hard and all he wanted to do was fuck her lights out at the time. He spread her booty with his hand and slid deeper in her guts causing her lips to tremble. He was feeding her pussy the entire nine inches and she was starting to cream turning his piece cocaine white.

"I feel it in my stomach," she cried placing a hand on his waist to slow him down.

He removed the dick from her warm kitty, rubbed it gently across her anus and eased inside. Before she could deny it, he locked both of her hands behind her and dug in deeply.

"Aghhh!" She gasped feeling the air leave her chest.

As he glided balls deep inside her, Peaches grunted before the tears began to fall down her face. "Tip—you—hurting me!" she shouted feeling her legs quiver.

"This what the fuck you wanted?" he replied showing no mercy.

After having his way from the back, Tipton pulled out and sat on the edge of her bed. "Get yo' ass on top of this motherfucker!"

After wiping the tears from her eyes, she squatted on him cowgirl style. He grabbed her by the waist and watched her ass bounce smoothly on his length.

"Daddy, it hurts?" she cried harder, as he began to slam inside of her. "I'm sorry—I'm so sorry."

Her ass clapped loudly against his pelvis and he could feel his nut approaching. He pushed her off him, then released his cum on her tongue.

"Swallow that shit," he demanded.

After regaining his energy, Tipton slid his pants back on. "I'm done with you, Peaches. I want you to stay away from me." He walked out of the bedroom.

"Tipton, don't do me like this," she pleaded before he closed the door behind him.

Peaches balled up against the bed and released the tears again. Her plea fell against deaf ears. Her emotions ran high as she sobbed through the rest of the night. After hearing his deep cutting words, Peaches made up her mind. If she couldn't have him, no bitch could. That was a fucking promise.

****

Making it to his home, Tipton quickly showered washing Peaches' scent from his skin. No matter how much he loved her, she made her own dirty bed and now it was time for her to sleep in it. After rinsing the water through his deep waves, he cut the shower off and stepped out. As he threw on some fresh clothes, his phone rang loudly. He picked it up off the bed and answered it.

"'Waddup?'"

"Nigga, you telling me to pull up on yo' spot. This bitch looks like a small movie theater. I'm at the front door," Rex said.

Tipton laughed as he hung up, then headed downstairs to let him in. Rex stepped pass the doorframe admiring the home. "So, this is what being rich feels like?"

"Trust me, I'm not there yet, in due time."

As they both took a seat on the living room couch, Rex tossed him a rolled blunt with a lighter. "Som how did things go with, Kimmi?"

"She enjoyed herself. I can't say the same for, Peaches." Tipton blew out a cloud of smoke.

"What, Ms. Drama Mama do now?"

"She was on some psyched-out shit with my baby. Like I had to kiss her ass in order to see her. I had to choke that silly ass girl out just for her to back up off me."

"So, after you was finna beat that ass, she let you slide with her?" Rex asked.

"Nah, I literally had to strap Kimmi in the car and pull off. I kept her til' like eleven and brought her back. She was so exhausted. After I dropped her back off, this bitch wouldn't let me out the door. She wanna pull me all to the room and get naked and shit. I grudge fucked her stupid ass and tore it down. That bitch is mental." Tipton smirked.

Rex stared at him with a funny expression, then leaned forward. "I know you ain't crank the DMX on that girl?"

Tipton covered his face. "You stupid as fuck man."

"It's yo' first night home and you crawled in Peaches booty like a spider."

"Like a lemur." He laughed.

"So, y'all back rocking or what?"

"Hell nah! I can't respect the shit she pulled while I was away. Spreading yo' legs while your man away is just nature, a venial mistake. Leaving me for dead is totally unacceptable. I can't trust nobody like that," Tipton confirmed.

"Smooth. So, what's the plan now? What you trying to do at this time, right here?"

Tipton puffed the Kush, then stood up. "I want my city back. You wanna learn how to whip or what?"

"Bruh, I been driving forever. It ain't nothin' you can teach me 'bout no car fool."

"Coke fool." Tipton gave him a pathetic expression.

"Like I told you before, I'm moving with whatever you touch. I'm paying attention. The only thing about that is it's gonna take more than just us bro."

Taking what Rex was saying into consideration, Tipton stared out his glass patio. "Leave that to me. These runners you got serving the weed. Do you trust them?"

"With my life," Rex responded.

"Good, I need you to ride with me today. I got to meet a few people. It's time to step it up a notch." Tipton placed the blunt in his ashtray.

"Smooth."

Chris Green

Chapter 10
8:00 a.m.

After Tipton and Rex picked Halo up from the prison facility, he wasted no time dripping his dawg in some of the best designer clothes. He put ten thousand dollars in his pockets before they stopped by Rex's crib to give him the last thing he desired. Two black, chrome 9mm handguns. Their timing was perfect because Jackson called just as they decided to head towards Tipton's crib.

"Waddup, Unc?"

"I'm texting you an address, I need you to pull up," his voice was stern.

"Say less."

Ending the call, Tipton jumped on the interstate. After typing the information into his GPS, he drove until his map system put him on a secluded back street. The gated home slightly resembled Tipton's. The only difference was the size and four, armed security guards. They wore all black and acted as if they were protecting the White House instead of a mini-mansion.

Tipton spotted Jackson in front of the doorway, pulled in and got out with Halo and Rex directly behind him. "Where the hell are we, Unc? This bitch surrounded like a navy base."

Jackson was accompanied by a man who stared at Tipton with a star-struck expression, catching him by surprise he embraced him into a tight hug. Tipton gazed at the stranger in confusion, he turned his attention to Jackson who stood with a wide grin.

"Am I missing something, do we know each other?"

Jackson looked him in the eyes and touched his shoulder. "Nephew, meet Vel, he's your father."

"It's a blessing to finally meet you, son. I can't tell you how many times I prayed for this day."

"Is this some type of fucking joke?" Tipton looked between both men.

"I know it may be hard to understand, right now, but after I found Jackson a few years back. He told me what was going on with you. All I could do was wait until you were released. I spent year after year begging Mary to let you come with me. I was denied every time. After you were born, she left me in Detroit and I never saw her again," Vel admitted.

Tipton roamed his eyes over at Jackson, who was nodding as if Vel's words were sincere. "I'm twenty-one years old and you just now coming around stressing that you're my father. I lost my mother at the age of thirteen and you still couldn't find me? What's the point of being here now?" Pain was laced in Tipton's tone.

"I can't make excuses for the past, Tipton. There were things going on that you were too young to understand. All I can ask for is a blessing on building a bond with you. For what it's worth, I truly missed you son. All I need is a chance to explain."

Shaking his head, he tapped Halo's arm. "I got business to attend to maybe another time," he replied, before heading back for the car.

"Just give him a little time." Jackson stepped over to Vel. "He's always been that way and I think this news is probably weighing kinda heavy on him."

"Sure," he replied with a heated expression while watching Tipton pull away.

****

"Maybe you should hear him out, Tip? He sounded like he was telling the truth," Rex suggested while playing away on his iPhone.

Refusing to reply, Tipton pushed the rest of the way in silence. There was absolutely no excuse that a man could give for staying away from his one and only son for twenty plus years.

He knew Mary would never do anything to hurt him. If she kept his father at a distance, it was obviously for a valuable reason.

"What time does this party start?" He looked over at Rex.

"We cranking up at nine o'clock sharp. This bitch 'bout to be exclusive." He grinned rubbing his hands together.

"Cool, let the games begin," he mumbled before gazing out at the beautiful city night. After today, he was about to make everyone think Queen Mary was alive in the flesh.

****

Club Mansion

As he stepped out of his McLaren, Tipton smoothed out his white *Dolce and Gabanna* two-piece suit and looked down at the *Fratelli Rossetti* chestnut loafers. Halo climbed out of the opposite side and guided him quickly into the VIP section of the club. The fellas slid past the bouncers and moved directly through the entrance. Live as always, the nightspot beamed with colorful lights. The entire dancefloor was packed, and beautiful women were moving around by the dozens.

Rex watched as Halo and Tipton headed over toward the private section, he instantly stood up on the couch with a bottle of Hennessey. "Y'all stand the fuck up for the man of the year. My motherfucking dawg. Welcome home, baby boy!" he yelled causing the VIP to applaud and cheer.

The spotlight was placed on Tipton, as the DJ did his special shoutout causing the club to scream in unison. "Welcome home!"

Tipton smiled from ear to ear, making his way up the small steps and pulled Rex into a bear hug. "Nigga where the hell did all these people come from?"

"Look around, bro. This is damn near the whole West Lake in this bitch."

Before Tipton could get another word out, he was gathered around by old classmates and past clientele. Even Ms. Berrett, the high school teacher showed up to wrap her arms around him. "I'ma let you have fun tonight, but me and you still have unfinished business." She slid her tongue across his neck.

"I guess, I'll be leaving with you then?" Tipton watched, as she walked off with her ass rocking to the beat.

The energy felt so wonderful seeing so many old faces brought back so many memories, as he tossed back a few drinks. Feeling a hand tug on his shirt, he turned around to see Peaches. She wore a tight-fitting dress and a pair of matching heels. Her honey-blonde hair was curled down her back and her cleavage protruded from the top of her dress.

"Hey, Daddy, you look good." She tried to kiss his lips. Tipton turned his face to dodge her and Peaches frowned. "I know we ain't finna start this? I told you I was sorry, Tip!"

"Cool, that don't mean I accepted your apology. I told you to stay away from me."

"Nigga, is you crazy? You think you just about to come home, fuck the shit out of me and leave? I'm warning you, please don't make me show my ass in here!" She was loud enough to grabbed the attention of all the guests.

As everyone started to give their undivided attention to them, Rex made his way over with a bottle in hand. "Peaches, not tonight. This is my event for bro and you ain't about to fuck it up. You need to leave."

"I ain't going nowhere. Fuck you flunky boy ass, nigga," Peaches snapped. "Tip, please don't try me like this 'cause you will regret it."

Taking a swig of his liquor, Rex nodded his head to the two bouncers standing behind her stepped in, grabbing her wrist, then they escorted her swiftly to the front entrance. "Get the fuck off me, bitch! I'm not going nowhere." They lifted her off the floor and carried her out kicking belligerently.

"She's gonna be trouble, I ain't never seen her act like this," Tipton said to Halo and Rex.

"Just let her be retarded, bro. She mad because you don't need her. She needs to go get her ass a job at K.F.C. or somethin', them folks hiring." Rex laughed before passing him a lit blunt.

"Speaking of the motherfucking devil, look at this nigga." Tipton tapped Rex, as Dejuan walked into the VIP.

Before he could get close, Halo placed a hand on his chest. "Who the fuck are you?"

"Nigga, don't ever put yo' hands on me. Are you crazy?" Dejuan shouted slapping his fingers down. Halo instantly reached for the gun on his hip, Tipton quickly grabbed his wrist. "It's okay, Halo, he's good." Halo tilted his head and his blue eyes grew wide before he stepped out of the way.

"Wassup, my nigga? When the fuck you start using security?" Dejaun shook his hand.

His eyes were fire red, you could smell the strong stench of liquor on his clothes. "He's just doing what he's paid to do. Waddup with you?"

"Nothing much, getting money as usual. Staying away from bustas." He cut his eyes to Rex.

"Be direct when you speak sideways, lil' nigga." Rex bit the remark quickly.

"Hold the fuck up. Don't come in here with that bad vibe shit. I been hearing you been on some real bullshit lately. Are you with us or against us? Because right now it looks like you on another team."

"What? Nigga, you been gone almost five years. Now you coming back like you the ruler of some shit. Just like I told him, I don't need nobody."

"What you here for then, Juan? Cause everybody over this way family." Tipton said.

"Family is just a word, I'm my own boss, nigga," Dejaun spat with arrogance before walking off.

"I told you that boy lost his damn mind. He ain't right?" Rex said as he watched him walk out.

"It doesn't matter anymore. Let's continue to have a good time and get to this money. We up next, with or without him."

"Smooth." Rex handed him the bottle.

The next few hours flew by with nothing but laughs and pure fun. Rex's private section was now overpacked and Tipton had gifts galore stacked against the couch as if it was his birthday. Spotting one of his old classmates, he embraced him into a hug.

"Long time no see," Sincere said, putting five grand in his palm. "Welcome back."

"It feels good to be back. How you been holding up out here in this world?"

Adjusting his Polo collar, Sincere grinned. "I'm trying to keep afloat. You know I'm too humble to fall under pressure."

"I got some good things in place, I'ma need a little help. You still down to make some paper?" Tipton questioned with seriousness.

"That's like asking me am I still alive."

"Say less, grab the info from Rex before you slide."

"Bet."

Sincere began to speak again, but his words started to fade as Tipton's eyes landed on a dark-skinned woman sitting alone on the couch. Her hair was light brown and pulled back into a ponytail. Her white embellished dress highlighted her beauty. Her healthy thighs were crossed giving a small view of her sexy legs, as she sipped lightly on a drink while the music bumped loudly.

"Are you alright?" Sincere turned his head to see what had, Tipton stuck.

"Her," that was all he could force from between his lips.

"That's my sister, Nita. She's a tough cookie to break, but she's single."

"May I?" Tipton asked as if he were a child begging for sweets.

"She's grown, my nigga. All I can tell you is good luck." Sincere gave him a pat on the back.

Feeling his heartbeat increase, he moved with confidence and took a seat next to her on the couch. "Hey, my name is Tipton. Do you mind if I join you, sweetie?"

As she gazed at him with her mystic hazel eyes, his stomach bubbled with nervousness. She was even more attractive up close. Nita's smile resembled *Gabrielle Union* and everything about her screamed wifey. Her almond-shaped eyes blinked with every move that Tipton made. Her chunky cheeks were a plus and her lips looked good enough to remove from her body. His eyes roamed up and down, Nita's frame as if he was ready to pounce on her like a lemur. She was all-out attractive.

"It looks like you made yourself quite comfortable," Nita replied.

Tipton flashed his dimples and rubbed his hands together. "I saw you sitting by yourself and just wondered could I keep you company? You are so beautiful," he uttered while staring at her like she was a movie actress.

"Thank you, that's very kind of you to say." She still vibed to the music.

"Are you having a good time tonight?"

"Not really, I don't really do the club thing. I just came out with my brother because he wanted me to get out of the house."

"I've known Sincere for a long time. I never knew he had a sister."

"Now you do." Nita sipped her drink.

"Is Nita your real name or is that short for something?"

Exhaling, she crossed her fingers and placed them on her knees. "Juanita."

"Are you really single?"

"Pretty much, never been a fan of the whole boyfriend thing." She smirked.

"A boyfriend is an understatement. You should be married and living in a big ole house with two kids, a dog, and a picket fence."

Nita giggled and shook her head. "What gives you that idea?"

"Look at you sitting over here all alone glowing like a trophy. All these dudes moving pass you to rush and dance with a groupie."

"Mhmmm, maybe I'm not that special," she said with a small smile.

"I'll cry if you ever say something like that ever again. I know a good girl when I see one."

Again, Nita smiled, looking up and down at his expensive clothing. "What do you do for a living, Tipton?"

She caught him off guard with the question, so he lied, "I'm an entrepreneur."

Nita chuckled and raised an eyebrow. "So, in other words. You're a bad boy, huh?"

"I wouldn't say bad, I'm very nice. I make people smile and always try to help everyone. I'm the man people can depend on if you're ever in need."

"Sometimes you have to focus on yourself to be the best you can be before you can help and attend to others."

Taking in her words, Tipton nodded. "What do you do? If you don't mind me asking."

"I attend Spelman College. I'm going for my doctrine degree in Psychology. I'm also on my last year for my master's in accounting. I have a part-time job at the Peachtree library to finish paying off my tuition and in my spare time, I paint," she replied.

"Paint?" Tipton's brow slanted. "Like what?"

"Portraits of my thoughts and feelings. I sell them online to keep me busy and to bring in a little more income."

"Maybe I can take you out and you can show me? I would love to see you express your talent," Tipton said in a genuine tone.

"Really?" She asked not knowing if he was serious.

"Why not? I think it's wonderful that you have a way to free yourself and show your feelings. I can take you to dinner and we can stop and get our paint on. That's only if you want to."

Thinking hard, Nita stared into his low brown eyes. "I'll need a little more time to think on it, Mr. Tipton. If you'll excuse me, I have to go to the ladies' room."

As he watched her walk off, he covered his mouth staring at her juicy apple bottom move softly from side to side.

"I know you ain't finna cry?" Rex asked from distance.

Tipton stood up and made his way over to him. "Bro, she literally made me fall in love in a matter of seconds, real shit."

"Sincere was just telling me how you was about to hang yo' self like a sick puppy. Was you able to grab her or what?"

"She didn't say yes, but she didn't say no either."

"Yeah, my nigga. She ain't no free pick. It's gonna take more than them pretty ass eyes of yours to tap that." Rex laughed hysterically.

"You a funny guy, I'm definitely not giving up." Tipton watched her disappear to the back.

He went back to engaging in a couple of conversations with a few good associates, time started to fly before he realized he hadn't spotted Nita within the past hour.

"Damn," he grumbled. "Yo', where Sincere at?" he asked Rex who was still indulging with a young woman.

"I think he left about thirty minutes ago, bro. It's about time for us to tear it down, too. It's almost one twenty."

Feeling like his world was over, he nodded for Halo so they could head out. "Excuse me, Sir." The bartender called him while looking at the trashed VIP section.

Tipton pulled two one-hundred-dollar bills from his pocket, walked over and placed them in his hand. "Sorry about the mess. Hopefully, this will cover your troubles?"

"Thank you. Sir, would you happen to know who is, Tipton?"

He looked at her funny eyed and folded his arms. "That's me. Why?"

"A young black woman who left a while ago told me to give this to you." She placed a napkin in Tip's hand.

Unfolding it, he smiled staring at Nita's name and phone number. It was guaranteed the best welcome home present he could have asked for.

Chapter 11

Tipton woke up to the doorbell ringing and rolled out of bed. The sun shined brightly through his window. Bundles of money was scattered on his floor and his head was thumping heavily from the liquor he consumed the night before. After making his way downstairs, he opened the door letting Jackson in.

"Rise and grind, baby boy. You look like you had the night of your life."

"You can say that." Tipton took a seat on the couch.

Jackson removed his shades and sat down across from him. "You know, you hurt ya father's feelings yesterday?"

Tipton laughed, then yawned and folded his arms. "I should be the one with the hurt feelings after twenty-one years."

"I know you might not wanna hear this, but my lovely sister, your mother, hasn't always been a kind sweetheart. Mary could get more heartless than a nigga at times when she was mad."

"And you say this because?"

"Because I want you to at least hear him out. Just cause he ain't been around doesn't mean he's lying about the way Mary kept you away from him. Vel has his hands tied in the dope game with an iron fist. He will be able to supply you with whatever you need. Why not take advantage?"

"Maybe that just ain't my way. I don't need nothing from him. I don't mind hearing what he has to say, but when it comes down to this business, I make my own way. I wanna meet my mama's plug like we agreed on," Tipton said.

****

South Dekalb Mall

Jackson, Tipton, and Halo entered a small restaurant, found a table for three and took a seat. "How're you gentlemen doing today? You fellas ready to order?" the male waiter asked.

"Not just yet. Does Rika happen to be in?" Jackson asked.

"Yes, she's in the back give me one minute." He headed behind the counter into the kitchen.

After a few minutes passed, Tipton spotted a slim Haitian looking woman stepping from the back, moving toward the table. She greeted Jackson with a hug, her hair was short, curly and dark red. Her bright skin made her mean gaze extra attractive, including the beauty mark that rested under her right eye. "Why're you surprising me at work? You know I'm busy."

"I got somebody I want you to meet, this is, Tipton." Jackson nodded over at him.

"Hi, Tipton." She winked after shaking his hand.

"That's Mary's son."

Looking back at him, she placed a hand over her heart. "Oh, my God! You look just like him. I haven't seen you since you were a child." Rika kissed his cheek and hugged him tightly.

"You know the apple never falls far from the tree," Jackson spoke. "He's here to speak business with you."

"Come with me." She smiled and grabbed his hand, leading him through the kitchen of the Picadilly's restaurant. Once they moved past the busy workers, Rika opened a small office door and pulled him inside. "I see you've grown into a handsome young man. Do you still have that little crush on me like you did when you were five?" She looked him up and down.

"I truly don't remember you. It's been a very long time. Jackson tells me that you were assisting my mother? I came to see if you can lead me in the right direction?" Tipton put on his business face.

Rika wrote down her cell phone number and placed it in his hands. "When you call, we speak in numbers, no words. Every call must end with, I love you and begins with, I miss you. It's my way of knowing it's you on the other end of the phone. One for twelve, if you buy more than five, it drops to ten apiece. I only move once a week. Every order means a different location which we will discuss after the first pick up. Any questions?" she asked to see if he could remember all the information.

"Nah, I want twenty. Whenever is good for you, I'm ready."

"Saturday, I'll meet you here to have dinner at six-thirty. Leave the money on your backseat and keep the driver's side door unlocked."

Tipton extended his hand to seal the deal, Rika grabbed the back of his head and forced her tongue into his mouth. She sucked gently on his bottom lip with a freaky kiss. "See you Saturday, big man." She giggled before letting him out of the office.

Feeling himself get aroused from her sexual antics, he hurried back to the front.

"Everything alright?" Jackson noticed the awkward look on his face.

"Yeah, we good to go."

"Rika, likes you, don't she?"

"I think she's just happy to see me," Tipton lied, as they made their way out of the mall.

****

Two Hours Later

After leaving his worker's spot, Rex stopped at the corner store for a pack of cigarillos. After greeting two familiar faces inside, he purchased his things and went back out.

"If it ain't the Waka Flocka rich boy?" Skeet stepped out of his escalade with four hittas behind him.

Rex gave him a quick smirk before ripping open his grape-flavored blunt. "What up, Mr. Sardine Man? Y'all niggas stay packed in a rental car every time I see y'all motherfuckers."

"Funny, I heard ya boy Tip made it home from the can. It's been a while," Skeet spat with a dirty smile.

Rex peeped the sneaky hand movements from his sidekick and pulled his Glock 40, just as the three men drew their weapons. "This just gotta be the day me and you die. Yo clique will

take the murders for both of us. Smile for the news dumbass."
Rex pointed at the recorder that rested on the corner.

"Clever, you hoe ass niggas always slide through the cracks
by the grace of God." Skeet waved his hand for them to stand
down.

"Maybe I just got good luck?"

"Do me a favor, will ya? Tell yo boyfriend, Tip that I've
waited four long years to get at him. I was hoping we can handle
this shit like men? So, I won't have to start popping innocent
bystanders like ya self."

"I'll see if I can get in contact with him."

"You do that," Skeet shot back.

Rex jumped into his B.M.W, smashed out of the parking lot
and dialed Tipton's number.

"You must've been reading my mind, bro. I was just about
to call you."

"Well, I'm damn sho glad you were thinking of me 'cause I
was just about to be involved with the next first 48."

"What?"

"I Just had a little run-in with ya boy, Skeet. Ain't no big-
gie."

"We can discuss that in a minute. I'm having a 101 in culi-
nary arts with a few employees at the spot, pull up."

"On the way." Rex hung up.

****

Twenty minutes later, Rex walked into Tip's home and
joined the small group in the kitchen. Everyone leaned around
as Chocolate took her turn at the stove with the glass Pyrex pot.
She reached inside to grab the rocks of cocaine, placed them on
a brown napkin and turned around with a smile.

"I told you I know what the fuck I'm doing," she bragged.

Tipton, Halo, and Sincere watched as she showed off her
skills.

"When you learn how to cook dope?" Rex asked coming out of his jacket.

Over the years Tipton was gone, Chocolate started to dip her fingers into the streets. Stripping, hustling, and gambling became apart of her everyday life. Her old skinny frame as a teen was replaced with a porn star body. Chocolate's young intentions were now fixated on counting dough.

"I learned after a dope boy started fucking me. This shit ain't free, nigga."

"Rex, it's on you, my guy." Sincere nodded towards the stove.

"I'm not gonna even waste my time. Fucking with me, we will have to re-up six times."

Sharing a laugh, Tipton walked into the center of them all. "He's right, at the end of the day everybody has a position to play. We all have to focus and understand that we're playing with some major league shit. This ain't no slap on the wrist, get out of jail type thing. People getting slammed with life sentences for blocks and I don't need that to be us. The way I see it, we spread out through the city and search for clientele who's in need of weight. I recommend you do yo' history on a motherfucker before you think of placing ties with that person. The whip game is where the profits come in. If we double, we all eat."

"So, let me get this straight. We can't deal with each other on the customers?" Sincere scratched his head. "What if I can't snatch the clientele, then what?"

"Then I suggest you migrate around the outskirts of Atlanta. There's no limit to how far we can go. It's all about smart decisions and calculated steps. If we're two steps ahead, nobody will be able to figure us out."

"That depends on where we're getting our shit, too. A lot of these fools out here stepping on bricks three times and asking for a twenty-five. It's not that easy." Rex chuckled.

"True, which is the reason why we serve people who are in need. If you got somebody that cop from you on the regular.

Watch and see how quick they come back for a re-up. If the purchases start to get a little too high, cut 'em off smoothly and let them know you're shutting down shop. A greedy person will do anything to win. Competition is easy and we got the fucking recipe." Tipton shrugged his shoulders.

"Well, I'm in, call when you're ready for me to move. I'm about to go shake this ass for some dollaz." Chocolate grabbed her purse to leave.

"Shit wassup? I got a lil hundred on me." Sincere stuck his tongue out seductively.

"Yo', Sincere. Are you sure that's the right information?" Tipton asked before he could leave out.

"I'm positive, you need to call her. I ain't never seen my sister smile like that. Just hit the line when it's time to take off." He walked out behind Chocolate.

"Say, God, I think you put together a nice team. Shit's gonna flow smooth, I can feel it." Halo sat on the couch.

"How in the hell did you get, Chocolate to stop by? That girl be in traffic more than a stoplight." Rex pulled the zip of weed out his pocket.

"I went to see, Kimmi and she was over there. After telling me what she'd been up to for these past few years, I asked her did she wanna make some money."

"And Peaches didn't say nothing?"

"You know I waited until I got the hell on to talk to that girl. We stopped at the gas station and traded numbers. Peaches, on the other hand, that girl really needs some help. She's so con-fused with life that it's crazy." Tipton placed his phone on the counter.

"It will all pass, my nigga. We dirty until the white man says we ain't, so let's grind til' we can't no more. And ya fuck ass homie Skeet tried to shine on me today. That boy really starting to irk my nerves." Rex tried to blow off the thought.

"You ain't got no location on that bum ass nigga?" Tipton mugged.

"Nah, the nigga got a few spots over by my worker on the Southside. They hang out at the store every now and then like they on some fake ass Nino Brown shit."

"Yo' Halo, you feel like riding out tonight?" Tipton was ready to squash the petty beef quick and quietly. As he leaned forward, his blue eyes glowed in excitement.

Chris Green

Chapter 12

11:37 p.m.

Rex spotted the Cadillac parked in the store's driveway, then parked across the street in front of the closed laundromat. "You see that busta right there in the black Polo shirt? That's the one who pulled the gun on me first. I ain't never seen the rest of them niggas." Halo nodded in silence, as he opened the door to step out. "You ain't taking the burner?" Rex asked after placing the gun on the seat.

Halo replied with a smile, placed the hoodie on his head and closed the door. He jogged lightly, making his way across the street. The three idiots in front of the store lingered, as he closed his distance. The knife Halo slammed into the first man's chest killed him instantly. Then he placed a solid punch to the next man's chin, he dropped allowing him to grab his last victim. Before he could pull the gun out of his sagging pants, Halo curved a hard, right fist into his throat. His body collapsed causing him to crash down onto the concrete.

Halo grabbed the gun and slung it into the street. He glared down at the man and started repeatedly delivering violent blows to the center of his neck. As Halo watched the blood spill from his nose and mouth, he finally released him. The smell of the man's bowels releasing told him his job was done. He stood looking around at his masterpiece, then trailed calmly back across the street, climbed in the car and glanced over at Rex who stared with a worried expression.

"Who the fuck are you, bro?"

Halo just grinned, reached over him and started the ignition. "Now would be time to pull off, God."

Rex came to the realization that Tipton sent him out with a psychopath and sped out of the lot leaving the crime scene in the rearview.

****

Tipton was laid back on his king-size bed, dialing Nita's number on his cell. After listening to the ring hum in his ear, she finally answered.

"Hello?" her voice sounded like an angel waking from her sleep.

"How you doing, beautiful? Did I catch you at a bad time?"

"No."

"Do you know who this is?"

"I'm quite sure I have an idea. No one calls my phone but family and work. How are you doing, Tipton?"

"I'm good now that I'm able to hear your voice."

"Really? I gave you my number twenty-four hours ago. You must've really wanted to talk," she said sarcastically.

"Dang ma, I didn't wanna be thirsty." Tipton cheesed.

"There's nothing wrong with showing someone that you have and see a great interest in them. That's the way to build a true connection. At least that's what my mom always said."

"Since you getting all political with the relationship facts. When am I gonna be able to get my date? I'm head over hills for you already, so we can skip that part."

"How you know I'm not still thinking on it?" Juanita spoke softly through the receiver.

"Because if you was, I would've known. I just asked you, baby."

Hearing silence for a few seconds, Tipton could tell she was blushing. "Why you all quiet? Over there smiling and stuff," Tipton teased.

"Are you outside of my bedroom door or something?" She laughed.

"I wish, I'm still stuck in my bed trying to get you to go out with me."

"I would love to go out with you, but I'm not really gonna have any spare time until next month. Work is kicking my butt and I can't afford to miss any days of school. It's like I'm always working or sleep."

"A month, I'm about to die man." Tipton mashed a pillow over his face.

"I understand if it's too long for you to wait. You're probably ready to push on and leave me alone now?"

"Me and you gon' end up fighting, Nita. I wouldn't care if your classes and work didn't end for the next twenty years. I'll be almost fifty waiting for my date."

"Tipton, that's just overboard." She giggled.

"Sometimes you gotta go overboard for what you want. If it takes a month to make you mine, I'm down with that, baby girl."

"Thank you, I look forward to you keeping your word."

"Always and you don't have to call me, Tipton. Everyone just calls me, Tip."

"But Tipton is your name, not, Tip."

Smiling at her sarcasm, he sat up on the bed. "Okay, Juanita."

"I see you got jokes tonight." She giggled into the phone.

"Just a few, I'm thankful for getting a moment of your time. Go ahead and take ya butt to sleep before you miss work. I'll call you tomorrow, beautiful."

"Goodnight, Tipton."

"Later gorgeous." He hung up.

Her voice, her demeanor, everything about her was an attraction to Tipton. It was beyond the small things in his past relationships. It was that feeling of a happy ending. As he pondered on the future, his doorbell rang. He headed downstairs and opened the door for Rex and Halo. After they stepped in, he secured the locks behind them.

"Any luck?" Tipton asked while heading into the kitchen for a shot of Hennessey.

"*Any luck*?" Rex repeated with a crazy expression. "Nigga, you sent me out here with this blue-eyed ninja cranking all kinds of Jet-Li stunts. Then you gonna ask a silly ass question like that? Who the hell is this man?"

"What the hell are you talking about, Rex?" Tipton thought he was exaggerating.

Halo sat down on the couch, grabbed the remote and found the channel two news. He turned up the volume and all three of them listened to the news reporter.

"Good evening, this is Johnathan Cochran with the channel two news. Currently on Alison Court in front of the abandoned White Cleaners. It appears we have two victims dead and one is in critical condition with a shattered jaw. As of now, there seem to be no witnesses and the cameras to the store are useless for a visual of the incident. There are no leads or suspects at this time, and detectives are doing everything they can to piece together this twisted story. We should have more tonight on the nine-o-clock news."

"Looks like a happy ending to me. Was anyone of them our lucky guy?" Tipton asked staring at the TV.

"No, but I damn sho' think he gon' know we've been there." Rex rolled some weed to ease his paranoia.

"Good, hopefully, he'll find something safe to do besides worrying about us."

Regardless of how Skeet played his cards, he was only gonna find one thing. A sweet first-class ticket to hellfire.

****

Tipton opened his eyes the next morning and stared at the clock that read 10:25 a.m. He jumped up in a rush, quickly brushed his teeth and hair, then found a clean set of casual clothes to put on. After choosing a white button-down, he grabbed a pair of slacks and matching loafers to finish off his magnificent swag. After heading out of the house, he drove to the four-star restaurant Houston's and placed an order of steak, triple cheese potatoes, and lemon pepper fish. Keeping a bird's eye view on the time, he stopped by the nearest Walmart and grabbed a dozen of white petal roses. After scooping up the meal, he made it down to the Peachtree library with ten minutes to spare.

Once he arrived at the building, Tipton conversed with Nita's boss for a second before she allowed him to enter. He proceeded up the flight of stairs, spotting her at the desk. Nita's face was buried in a stack of paperwork. The area was extremely quiet, and citizens moved around checking out books and logging into the computer systems. Tipton strolled forward and moved unnoticed until he stood in front of her. "Ma'am, do you know where I can find, Ms. Stanton?"

Before she could reply, Nita looked up into Titpon's face with a huge smile. "Are you known for popping up on people while they're at work?"

"Only when they are too busy and don't have enough time to step out. These are for you." He handed her the roses.

"They're beautiful, you're so sweet." She placed her nose up to the delicate roses.

"Come on, I brought you lunch." Tipton held out his hand for her to stand up.

"I can't just abandon my post, Tipton, I'll get in trouble."

"Not according to your, boss lady. I just talked to her downstairs and she happens to be Benjamin Franklin's number one fan. We got one hour."

Nita shook her head, stood and grabbed his hand. "You are so stubborn."

"It's your fault." He laughed.

Tipton led her to the outside deck where the readers occupied their laptops, found a table and placed the trays down with a bundle of napkins. "I hope you like steak and fish. I didn't wanna take any chances of being late, so I ordered the best thing on the menu."

"Did you plan this?" she asked after he took a seat in front of her.

"Kinda, I mean, I just jumped up and tried my luck. I guess I'm just a natural winner." He pinched one of her cheeks.

Tipton's devotion to make her smile was a gigantic step into their new friendship. Nita truly didn't know what she was feeling for the young man, who popped into her life out of the blue. All she could hope was that his words matched the actions and sincerity along their quest.

"Can I ask you something?" She took a bite of her fish.

"Shoot."

"You look like you have great business about yourself. You're very handsome and genuine. You probably could have any woman you want. Why me?"

Tipton bit a piece of steak, wiped his mouth and sat down his fork. The look in her hazel eyes alerted him that the question was picking at her brain.

"I was raised by my mother. I never grew up with my father. Her love and strive was the fuel to my heart. She showed me care that I've never felt. Women are gentle creatures, but some can be savages like most men. I try my best to treat a woman like my mother treated me, with love. So, with that being said having just any female isn't what I want. A queen is something I need."

"I bet your mother is proud of how you're carrying yourself."

"I guess."

"You guess? I think that's a fact, I hope I can meet her one day."

"She's dead."

Feeling her heart drop, she placed a hand over her chest. "I'm so sorry, I didn't mean—"

"It's okay, ma. She was killed in front of me on my thirteenth birthday. In my mind, showing and giving love is the only way I feel she can still live through me," Tipton uttered while picking back up his fork.

"From your actions, I can tell she was a good woman." Nita placed a hand over his.

"Thanks, beautiful. What about you, though? It still shocks me that you aren't seeing anyone."

Nita shrugged and twirled her fork around in the potatoes. "I tried once when I was in high school. A man who I fell in love with cheated and left me as if I was a lousy second prize project. A lot of dudes were intimidated to talk to me, and it sent me into a slight depression. I started to feel like there was something wrong with me. I eventually blocked out the entire relationship thing and decided to focus on my goals and dreams. And here I am," she said as if her life was pathetic.

Tipton leaned over and placed a hand under her chin. "You are the most gorgeous woman I have ever met in my life. You damn sho' ain't no lousy project. And there is absolutely nothing wrong with you. I don't plan on going anywhere just to let you know." Tipton stared at her with passion pumping through his pupils.

Nita blushed from ear to ear, stood up and placed a chaste kiss on his cheek. "I have to get back to work, love. My papers are stacked to the ceiling. I will be expecting a phone call from you tonight, Tipton." She glowed with joy while running her French manicured fingertips through his waves.

"Always, baby girl," he said before she stood up to head back inside.

Nita's hair blew with the light breeze and the jeans she wore hugged her curves to perfection. She was everything and more. It was a must, Tipton wouldn't stop until Juanita Stanton was Mrs. White.

Chris Green

Chapter 13

24 Hours Later: Saturday

After counting the two-hundred grand, Tipton placed it in bundles of five thousand, dropped the rolls into a handbag and headed out for the car.

"When we get there, just keep your eyes open. If we think anything doesn't feel right, you know what to do." He looked at Halo, who was sitting behind the wheel of Rex's B.M.W.

"Understood, God." He rolled up the window.

Tipton climbed into his vehicle, placed the money in the backseat and pulled off. Thirty minutes later the guys were pulling into the South DeKalb mall and plaza. Tipton parked his car a few spaces down from Halo, then cut off the ignition. He sat the money in the passenger seat, got out and headed inside the Piccadilly restaurant.

As he walked inside, Tipton looked around before spotting Rika sitting in a booth by herself. As he headed over, she smiled and he took a seat. Her work uniform was replaced with a brown and black, high-end dress that stopped at the middle of her thighs. Her pretty feet sported a pair of three-hundred dollar, *Chanel* flip flops and her red hair was nearly curled brightening her facial features.

"Hello, handsome." She hugged him.

Tipton pecked her cheek with a light kiss and nodded. "Waddup, Rika?"

Before she could reply, a waiter arrived at the table with a full course meal. As he stared at the steamed broccoli and cabbage with a dish of baked chicken and macaroni, Tipton's stomach began to grumble.

"I hope you're hungry?"

"Hell yeah, I ain't put nothing in my system all day." He grabbed some silverware.

"Thank you for being on time. It shows a lot of consideration with my job."

"No problem, ma, it's business. Being on point is the only way I know," Tipton agreed.

"Your mother was the same way. I've never met anyone like her when it came down to this game. She taught me a few things that has taken me a long way."

"It's crazy that you say that. So many people have told me stories about, my mama. They damn near make me think she was hustling harder than these rich ass niggas running around the city?"

"What makes you think she wasn't?" Rika sipped on her glass of water.

Looking at her stern expression, Tipton could tell the remark was a serious one. "The same niggas running around here today living the life was on your mama's payroll at a certain point. She was the true Queen of the city. No one was doubling a key and selling it for the original price like Mary. She was so good our plug dropped the prices down to a number that'll give you a heart attack."

Listening to her words about his mother's success forced him to grin. "So, who is this lucky plug?"

"In due time," Rika smirked.

She grabbed his hand, pulled it under the table and stuffed it between her legs. Feeling his fingers touch her bare pussy lips, they instantly became drenched from the slippery cookie between her thighs. "I knew you was gonna grow up to be a boss," Rika mumbled seductively. Observing his speechless face, Rika leaned over to his ear. "It feels even better when you're inside it."

"I believe you," Tipton whispered with his head down. His fingers were still swimming around in her kitty.

"Our next location is the movie theater in Atlantic station. The same rules, same time. Call me to place your order." She squeezed his manhood twice.

"Thank you, Rika." He stood up and grabbed a napkin to wipe his fingers.

After kissing his cheek, Rika giggled lightly knowing it was only a matter of time before he would crack.

****

Tipton headed back out to the car, jumped in and stared at the large Piccadilly food box resting on his seat. Opening it up, he glared at the perfectly wrapped kilos and smiled. Rika was truly the definition of a real plug.

Tipton cranked up, pulled out and gave a thumbs up to Halo. Swerving out directly behind him, they exited the parking lot and headed back for the house. Tipton picked up his phone and quickly called Rex.

"Wassup, my guy?"

"Waddup, fool, is everyone over there?"

"Yep."

"The girls, too?"

"Yeah, they here, but I might eat both of they lil' fine asses before you can get back."

"Cool, I'll be there in a minute."

"Smooth." Rex hung up.

****

As he walked through the house, Sincere sat on the couch conversing with Chocolate, and Rex entertained Tipton's two first day home showgirls.

"Anybody ready to work?" He asked moving into the kitchen where the table of equipment was set up.

Everyone made their way inside, as Tip dumped the twenty bricks of cocaine on top of the stove. "Chocolate, do ya thang," he said before stepping out of the way.

Chocolate cracked her fingers, picked up the two cloth masks and gave them to the female workers. "Y'all gonna need these, get undressed."

Chocolate put on her own mask, pulled her shirt off and tossed it on the living room floor. Then she unbuttoned her pants, pulled them off and did the same. She now stood in front of the boys with no bra and a thong that sunk between her booty cheeks, they stared with lust pumping from their pants.

"Damn, Chocolate, where the hell you get all that ass from? You was skinny as a damn straw in school."

"Fuck you, Rex." She stepped into the kitchen with the two women behind her waiting for instructions.

Chocolate cranked up the stove, grabbed two Pyrex pots and began explaining to the girls what needed to be done. In a matter of minutes, Tipton, Rex, Halo, and Sincere watched as the chemistry lab jumped into effect.

Being sure to keep his eyes on the time, Tipton turned on the A.C when the heat began to rise through the home. Sincere prepped the work as the girls moved like Shaq and Kobe in the nineties. For some reason, Tipton couldn't help but observe Chocolate and her whip game. The pace of her movements. It looked like she was born to be in the game. Right then, he knew she was going to be his number one business partner.

****

One Month Later

As he pushed his new 2015 Landrover down the street, Tipton nodded his head to *Jay-Z* and *Beyonce's* single, '*Drunk In Love.*' The sun was sitting high at eighty degrees and the beginning of May was vastly approaching. Money was sitting extra pretty in his lane. Chocolate was making so many plays that he had to purchase a few counters in order to keep it all together. Her connections shot from four to nine in a three-week span. Her whip game was getting more fantastic and the ounces people were buying eventually turned into shipments of blocks. The entire city wanted the product he was toting. He dialed Rika's number, the phone rung once before she picked up.

"Hello?"

"I miss you," he replied through the receiver.

"I miss you, too."

"Forty, I love you."

"I love you, too," she responded in a sexy tone before ending the call.

At the time, shit just couldn't get any better. His first real date with Nita was tomorrow and their late-night conversations only made him crave her more. Their bond grew closer as the days passed, now it was time to show her that he was the one to settle for.

As he rode past his old neighborhood, he thought about Lisa. It had been four years since she spoke to him. No letters, no visits. The last encounter between them wasn't good, but it was never a point where he would turn his back if she was in a critical condition.

As he turned down her street, Tipton decided to stop by and do a quick check-in. Looking at the grass in front of the house, reminded him of an abandoned home. It was clear that Lisa didn't try to give a shit after he'd decided to leave.

Tipton stepped out of the car and made his way to the door. He knocked twice, then twisted the knob and walked inside. Lisa was asleep on the couch with her television blaring as if she was deaf. Her coffee table was cluttered with trash and her clothes smelled like they hadn't been washed in forever.

Tipton cut off the TV, moved to the couch and woke her with a slight nudge.

Lisa opened her eyes and sat up. "Tip, hey baby. When did you get out?" her voice was sore and weak.

"What happened to you, Lisa? Why does the house look like this?"

"I just gotta straighten up a bit." She stood to her feet with a tired expression.

All her weight had vanished. Her mocha skin now resembled a dried peanut brittle. Black bags covered the bottom of her eyes and her breath smelled horrible.

"Tip, let me give you a blowjob for a little co-pay, baby. You know I won't tell nobody." She reached for his pants.

Tipton grabbed her hand tightly, looked down at the table and spotted a crack pipe. He slowly picked it up and put it in her face. "What the fuck is this, Lisa? You smoking now? Who the fuck gave you this shit?" Tears were sitting in the corners of his eyes.

Even though Lisa wasn't blood, she still held a place in his heart as an auntie. She was his mother's best friend and that held more weight than anything.

"How you gon' be mad at me when you left me alone? Juan gave it to me since you trying to treat me like a child, Tipton. Be mad at him and tell that motherfucker he ain't trapping out of my house no more unless I get some co-pay." She folded her arms.

Hearing Dejaun's name made his heart crack to pieces. Trust, loyalty, and friendship. All the fake ass terms he could think of went out of the window as rage tingled through his chest.

"Let's go." Tipton pulled Lisa out of the house towards the car.

He put her in the passenger seat, got in and swerved off. After driving for about twenty minutes, he pulled inside a nearby rehabilitation center.

"What the hell am I supposed to do here, boy? This one of those slave houses?" Lisa fussed while folding her arms forcefully.

"It's a place that will help you get better, auntie. Don't you want my help?"

"Help me with some damn money, and take me back home," she grumbled.

Tipton placed a hand on her shoulder. "If you do good here, I'll move you away and make sure you're good. You have to work with me, Lisa."

Twisting up her face, she fumbled with her decision before agreeing.

After taking her inside, Tipton pulled two-grand from his pocket and gave it to the woman behind the counter.

"This is my auntie, and she needs help. Whatever the treatment runs, I'll double it for her to stay supervised at all times."

Giving him a distraught look, she nodded. "She'll be fine. You can come back tomorrow and fill out the paperwork for her."

The worry in his eyes showed that he cared for her. "Thank you."

"Tip, this isn't my home. Don't leave me here," Lisa begged.

"Tomorrow I will be back, I promise you will be okay. You have to trust me."

As he turned to leave out of the center, he called Rex. "Wassup Brodie?"

"Meet me at the spot, now!"

"Is everything smooth, bro, what happened?"

"I want you to take me to wherever, Dejaun, is at."

"I'm on the way now."

Tipton hung up the line, jumped in the car and sped off.

****

While eyeing Peaches naked in the bed, Dejuan pulled up his pants and stared at her large behind. "Go ahead and clean up girl." He rubbed the top of her back.

Smiling, she stood up and kissed his lips. "Are you still gonna give me the money to go shopping next week." She rubbed on the center of his chest.

He pulled eight-hundred dollars from his pocket and placed it in her hand. "I'm about to head over to the spot. Don't go nowhere cause I'm coming back."

"I got you, Daddy."

Dejuan left out of the bedroom and walked pass Tipton's daughter who sat on the floor watching cartoons. "Daddy will be back, Kimmi." He laughed to himself before leaving the house.

****

Dejuan arrived on the Southside and pulled his car through Ashley Court apartments. Besides the few people he normally kicked it with in the area, it was a great late-night spot to hustle if you needed extra cash.

He parked his whip, got out and headed towards the small crowd that posted up along the sidewalk. The complex was known to keep a freak or two, so being bored was out of the question. His mind was so distracted, he never paid attention to Tipton walking up on him.

Tipton grabbed his shoulder, spun Dejuan around and landed a hard, right fist to his jaw. Dejuan fell on his ass, then staggered to get up while looking up at his childhood friend.

"Nigga, is you stupid? You gave my auntie dope!" Tipton kicked him in the side of his face.

People started stepping out of their apartment witnessing the brutal beating. "Fight back pussy ass nigga." He gave Dejuan space to stand up.

Dejuan's mind was so discombobulated, all he could do was reach for the gun on his waist. Tipton quickly grabbing his wrist and crashed a violent elbow across his chin sending him back to the ground. Rex kicked the gun, snatched it up and hurried to stop the catastrophe.

"I gave you whatever. You was supposed to be, my dawg." He kicked Dejaun forcefully in the mouth.

"Tip, that's enough, bro. You gon' kill him." Rex stepped in front of him.

"Fuck that, nigga! I go to prison and you put my auntie on crack. Out of all these motherfuckers you serving in the street?"

Dejuan staggered to his feet, listening to Tipton's words as blood dripped swiftly down his face.

"I'm warning you, Juan. That was the last strike. If you violate me or my family again, yo' bitch ass gon' need more than a gun to stop me from you killing you."

Dejuan blinked his eyes in confusion, as Rex retreated with Tip back to the car. All Dejuan could do was mug both of them until they exited the apartments.

"Juan, you a'ight, my nigga?" A distant voice asked.

Ignoring the question, he walked slowly back to his whip and slid into the driver's seat. "Fuck!" He slammed his fist down repeatedly against the dashboard.

Feeling his head throb in pain, Dejuan drove off devising a plan for revenge. It was a ghastly mistake when Tipton didn't finish the job and left him breathing. The entire time he wanted to mend the relationship with his friend, it turned back to bite him. The war was officially on.

Chapter 14

After picking up, Kimmi, Tipton, and Rex headed back to the house for a few rounds of blunts and Hennessey. "He's gonna be a problem, I can feel it," Rex stated rubbing his chin. "You did him too wrong, Tip."

"And he deserved it. The entire time we've been friends, I never pulled grimy on that nigga, not once. Lisa is my family, that's like me going over to his mom's house, making her suck my dick for some paper. If you pull a conniving ass stunt like that on yo' fam, you ain't never have no love from the jump."

"True, but these are also signs, that we already saw when we were younger. The nigga is just an all-around fuck up. He's meant to be alone."

Tipton stood up and put his glass in the kitchen sink. "At the end of the day, I'm done with all the nice guy shit. If he wants smoke, then I ain't got no problem handling his ass. The way I look at it, he was just another problem in our way. Shit has been perfect, I ain't never made this much money in my life. I don't have the tolerance for any bullshit, right now."

Hearing his words, Rex smirked. "Things will all fall into place boss man. Just relax and let the operation take its course."

Tipton just sat back and thought to himself. *Disloyalty always has a funny way of exposing itself. Whether it's through words or actions. Betrayal was a trait you could never hide. It was the reason hustlas like himself lasted in the game. Loyalty would equal wealth and anything opposite would surely mean death. It was just the life of a dope boy.*

****

The Next Day

It was three o'clock in the evening when Tipton pulled into his driveway with Nita right by his side. As Nita stepped out of his car she looked at the large home in amazement.

"You must've worked pretty hard to get a house like this?" She took his hand as they moved around to the backyard.

"I put in some, my family played a big part also." Tipton opened the gate to walk around his property.

As her eyes landed on the huge yard, Nita smiled. A large painting set up was ready and prepped for use. Thirty different colors of paint sat along the grass and over twenty white poster boards were hanging on numerous wooden stands. The choice of paintbrushes rested on the table that faced out towards the pond.

"And who is this little cutie?" Nita asked as Kimmi made her way over with a picture in hand.

"Daddy, I'm finished." She grinned handing it to him.

"Nita meet my daughter, Kimmi. Baby girl, this is daddy's girlfriend."

"Hi, Ms. Nita." She waved and walked over to Rex who was chilling by the backdoor.

"Oh my God, she is so precious. I love her!"

"She's four, besides her, you and a couple of my friends is all I got." Tipton led her over to the painting equipment. "You talked a good game about what you can do with that brush. I think I can give you a run for it." He challenged picking up a brush.

"Oh really? What makes you so confident?" Nita grabbed an apron and placed it around her body.

Taking a step back, Tipton gave her a look, as if she'd insulted him. "Girl you ain't know, I'm too nice with that pen. I'm probably even better with this."

"You're on." She picked up her brush.

Within minutes of starting their piece, Nita was engrossed in her work. Her eyes were glued to the masterpiece that was being created. Her head tilted every time her brush touched the paper like she was searching for perfection.

Tipton couldn't help but glance at her beauty while she worked. Her tongue would slightly protrude from her lips every thirty seconds. Her legs shifted from side to side showing off her hypnotizing curves and hips. Nita's attractive hazel pupils widened with every stroke her arm took. The sight of her was just irresistible.

Catching him in the staring act, Nita flashed a sexy smile. "I hope you got something on your paper by now? We're twenty minutes in and I haven't heard no trash talk from you yet."

"I got a lil' sum-sum." He chuckled while looking at the board in front of him.

"Well, let's see it." She folded her arms with a smirk.

"I don't think so, Miss Artist, you first."

"Okay," she nodded and sat down her brush. Then turned the board around.

Tipton gazed at the astounding portrait of a man and woman silhouette kissing as the sunset. "Yo' that shit ain't fair. You just got down on me." Tipton looked at his paper with a fake attitude.

"Nah, *Mister I'm too nice with the pen.* Turn it around so we can see what you got it."

As Tipton turned his board around, she heaved over in a fit of laughter after viewing the stick figure he painted. "Go ahead, get ya joke on." He nodded.

"Aww, Tipton that's a beautiful piece. You won that hands down." She pulled him in for a hug.

"Let's go eat, that ain't the only stuff I got drawed up. The rest of my work is just in the house."

"You gotta show me your portfolio sometime." Nita giggled.

Grabbing ahold of her hand, Tipton led her through the patio door inside the kitchen. They walked into the living room where their meal was set, Nita froze in place with a hand covering her mouth. She took a second to look at his wall, it was decorated with all her recent paintings that were for sale.

"I told you I had better stuff inside." He pulled her chair out so she could be seated.

"You bought all of my work," She mumbled in a soft tone.

"I couldn't beat that. Five hundred dollars apiece for fourteen memories that'll last a lifetime was well worth it."

As she sat down at the table she gazed into his eyes.

"What?"

"I can't believe you really did this."

"Why not? Your artwork was online to be sold, ma. I feel sorry for the people who couldn't order in time."

"Thank you." She rubbed his hand.

He lifted her fingers to his mouth and kissed them delicately. "No need."

After sharing their wonderful meal of sauteed shrimp, grilled shish kebabs and fried lemon chicken, they retired to the couch to watch the classic movie *Love and Basketball.*

Nita laid on his chest and stared at him. "What makes me different from any other woman?" She wanted to see where his mind was.

Tipton paused the movie and licked his lips. "Your beauty. The way you understand life and move through this world to make it fit for you. Your attitude and the strive and passion you hold for a talent you aren't afraid to express. There's many things I can call out to give you a certain uniqueness," he said with assurance.

"Do you feel that I'm a good friend to you?" Her finger twirled on his chest.

"Without a doubt. Nita, I don't just bond with women for something to do. I try and build friendships that will last a lifetime. I'ma spill you a lil' drank so you can be on game. If you ever have to second guess with anyone about anything, you don't need 'em, friend or lover. Women dedicate their time and energy to a person they know are full of lies and deceit. It's because their too scared to adhere to the truth. They've been done wrong for so long, that settling for it is the only option.

Every person deserves a true friend. But sometimes you gotta scratch the surface to rise and find them."

Respecting his choice of words, Nita rested her head back against his chest. "Do you think I would make a good wife?" she uttered waiting for a response.

"Only if you marry me," he responded seriously.

Adjusting on the couch, she placed her leg around him. "Why do say that?"

Their faces were now close together and they were breathing softly in each other's personal space. Tipton kissed her gently and she nibbled on his upper lip. "Because another man wouldn't know how to treat you. And if I can't have you, nobody can." Tipton smoothed a hand across her cheek.

His statement caused her heart to slightly speed up. "Okay," she replied not knowing what else to say.

After making out for the fourth time, Nita's panties were soaking wet. The urge to take him on the couch was pumping through her body. It just wasn't a stage she wanted to indulge in yet. When Tipton promised her it would never be a rushed priority. They finished their movie and he drove her home. His feelings were starting to reach the max with Nita. Her style and entire character was what caused him to want her more. It was guaranteed that if she kept the happiness instilled, she would be the one reciting the special words, *I do.*

$$****$$

As he pulled back in his driveway, Jackson leaned against his new black Jaguar.

"Waddup old man?"

"You, what ya got planned for the rest of the day?"

Looking at his watch that read seven-thirty, Tipton shrugged. "Nothing. You got some in mind?"

"I wanna take you over to ya father's spot. He wants to speak to you about something."

Smirking, Tipton folded his arms. "You just don't quit do you?"

"All you have to do is listen. I wouldn't ask you to if there wasn't something on the table for you to benefit from." Jackson tried to reason with him.

When Tipton climbed into the passenger side of the car, Jackson smiled and got inside. "Trust me, rich boy. This will satisfy your taste buds for the paper."

Instead of answering back, Tipton prepared for what lied ahead.

****

Jackson and Tip got out of the car at Vel's extensive crib and headed for the door. "Please don't be all uptight, nephew. He's still your dad."

"Yeah, whatever," he replied before they were let in.

"Glad to see that you boys could make it. How you doing son?" Vel held his hand out.

"Perfect," he said giving him a firm shake.

Observing Vel's wardrobe, Tipton could tell he was an old dude with flavor. He rocked a Burberry shirt with matching jeans. They were custom-designed with the bleach patterns aligned by the pockets. The sight of his Timberland boots gave him the swag of an up north nigga. If it wasn't for the salt and pepper in his goatee, he could easily go for thirty instead of forty-two.

"You fellas want something to drink?" Vel asked as they moved into the massive living room.

The decor of his home was laced with expensive furnishings. You could tell that a professional's touch was invested and dedicated to making his home topnotch.

"Sure," Jackson answered for both of them.

"Sonya!" Vel called out in a stern voice.

A woman dressed in all black made her way into the living room and waited for his instructions. Her hair was frizzy, and her hands were folded behind her back as if she was about to salute her commander.

"Yes, sir?"

"Could you please grab three glasses of Scotch with no ice for me?"

Without replying, Sonya turned to retrieve his request. Not only did Tipton peep her large amount of ass, but he scoped the handle of a black Glock resting in the center of her back. Logging it in his memory card, he continued to relax like everything was normal.

"Tipton. I know me and you haven't really had the chance to unite and sit down for a discussion. Your uncle tells me you're a busy man?"

"I have my moments," he stated arrogantly.

Sonya walked back in with their drinks, handed them all a glass and departed from their presence. "Listen, son, I know you may have some ill feelings against me for not being there. No matter what I tell you, it still won't fix the time that has passed. The only thing I can do is look forward to building a better relationship for our future," Vel spoke with respect.

"I'm a big boy now, emotions are something I don't carry. When I grew up without you, I learned a few things. The first was to never count on anyone, not even family. Second, never cage in feelings for shit that ain't making me no money." Tipton downed his liquor.

Bobbing his head in approval, Vel stood up. "I think that's a strong trait in our blood. Money makes the world float and we have nothing without it. I learned that at a young age like yourself. It's the reason I called you here today. I want to offer you a proposition. You're in a spot where you can help me and in return, I'll pay you for the services."

"Maybe you need to be a little clearer, I don't understand."

Jackson sipped his drink as they continued to talk.

"Of, course, you know I have a large and profitable business in place. Chop shops, weapons, and drugs. I know you have the skill to cook. With my supply and your wrist game, we would be able to lock down the entire city. If long enough, the entire state. My plug guarantees me fifty kilos a month and I distribute it to the workers to break down. I want you to come work for me. Just to show you I'm not asking for a handout. That is what I'm placing in your possession. To show you that I mean business." Vel grabbed the huge duffle and placed it in the center of the floor.

"What's that?" Tipton asked with a raised brow.

Vel unzipped it and slid it closer. "Two hundred and fifty thousand dollars, cash. It's yours, all you have to do is agree to work with me. When the ball starts rolling, I'm willing to split profits with you sixty forty, no one loses." He attempted pulling out a bundle of money.

"No, thank you."

"Excuse me." He laughed before looking at Jackson confused.

"I'm Gucci, the game is meant to be sold, not told. I have my own plug. I've made three hundred and thirty thousand in the past month. That was only using half of what you coping. It's not worth it. No disrespect, but I'm my own boss. And if anybody working, they gon' be under me. Not the other way around." Tipton stood out of his chair.

"You not gon' even give it a chance before you turn me down? I mean you're a so call money-getter. I just put a quarter-million dollars in your face, and you're saying no?" Vel asked with anger.

"Exactly, that paper don't mean shit. And I'll say it again, I got my own money. So, no, if I give up my recipe, I give away my hustle. Everything I earn on this side is a hundred percent profit. I have my own crew dispersing on every side of the city and I've been doing just fine. So, I'm gonna have to turn down your offer."

"Tipton, that's like a slap in my face. I'm your father and I'm trying to show you that I wanna be apart of this as a team. You're turning me down?"

Seeing where the conversation was leading, he walked away and headed for the front door. Jackson held up a finger for Vel to calm down, then followed Tipton out of the house.

"I don't understand. Is something wrong?" He stopped Tipton in his tracks.

"Nigga, how the fuck this man know I can whip? I ain't even had three conversations with this guy and he got his nose all in my business."

Jackson walked closer and folded his arms. "I just saw a good avenue where you can lock down the game from all angles. I never intended for you to get mad or think I'm telling him anything about your setup, Tipton."

"What don't you get about me not liking this dude? His entire energy is crooked. I've never met this man in twenty plus years. Now he wants to come around when I'm grown and ask me how to cook coke? This nigga ain't asked me nothing about what I've been through. What's my favorite football team? Nothing! He's trying to use me and unfortunately, I'm not foolish. So that nigga needs to find another sucka to play with?" Tipton yelled.

"You gotta stop thinking that everybody is out to get you, man. You can't make all the money in the world by yourself nephew."

"I don't need all the cash in the world. I just need enough to say I did my fucking job. Get me the fuck away from here." He stormed off to the car.

Stepping out on the porch, Vel mugged Jackson. "What the fuck is that lil' nigga's problem?"

"You just gotta give him time. You've been away all his life. It's kinda hard for him to adjust, right now. I'll get up with you when things smooth out."

Vel stepped off the porch to leave. "Yeah, you do that," he mumbled.

Vel only knew one thing, the city wasn't big enough for competition. It took him forever to reach his spot and it surely wasn't going to be challenged by no one. Not even his son.

Chris Green

Chapter 15

Rex pulled into the parking lot of Chocolate's three-bedroom working house, he and Tipton stepped out of their cars, glancing at the new cameras she'd installed, then they proceeded to the door. After knocking hard on the burglar bar gate, they patiently waited.

"One second, yall," A voice spoke through the small speaker by the doorbell.

They looked at each other and shared a laugh before Sincere let them in. "My niggas, how y'all boys feeling today?" He greeted them both with a handshake.

"We a'ight, I thought Chocolate might've had a robot running the spot with all this weird-ass technology we got going around this bitch?" Rex stared at the table of cocaine.

"You can thank Tipton for that. This man got this girl thinking she's Big Meech and shit. I think she tried to manhandle me yesterday," Sincere replied, as they stepped inside the kitchen.

Chocolate sat at the large table counting bills with a pair of thin rubber gloves, the windows behind her was boarded down and a metal pole was mounted in front of the backdoor indicating that no one was allowed through it.

"Wassup, baby girl. What the hell you about to do, base a turkey?" Rex asked looking at her gloves.

Chocolate rolled her eyes and remained quiet until counting the last bill. "For your info silly ass nigga. I'm tired of getting paper cuts on my damn fingers. Maybe you need to try adding some to yours." She said standing up.

Rex stared down at her Georgia peach, then pinched it lightly. "Don't touch if you ain't spending fifty thousand dollars, nigga." She slapped Rex's hand down.

"Shit, that must gon' cover me for a lifetime supply." He laughed.

Ignoring his actions, Tipton stared in her eyes. "You a'ight?"

"Yep, that's seventy-five. I already took out my twenty and we still got four in the living room." She slid the bundles of cash across the table.

"Say less, ma, that's cool." Tipton thumbed through the paper.

"I think we need to think about another spot. I been having to come way across town just to re-up. Twenty keys ain't enough," Sincere stated.

"I was just about to say the same thing, Tip. I practically sold two in a half just today. All that was in straight zips. That shit is pure raw," Chocolate agreed.

"That's the reason I came to talk to y'all. Shit is moving faster than I expected, so the money I paid y'all this month is probably about to double. I'm upping the supply for our next round, so we might need a few more people. Meisha and Keisha can't keep cutting that shit alone. Also, me and you can't be the only two who know how to cook." He looked at Chocolate.

"Now that you mention those two. Did they really put that West Coast production orgy down on you that day you came home?" Rex was rolling a joint with a stupid grin.

"Anyway," Chocolate interrupted. "What are you trying to tell us?"

"I'm saying teach the girls how to whip and hire someone else to cut and bag the product. They been around since we first started. It ain't no reason they don't know by now. We can't afford to get tangled up with time and work ourselves. We gotta leave room for our personal business. And not only that but to network with more buyers. If it can keep flowing like this, we will start seeing every bit of five hundred grand a month."

"I'm glad that you mentioned buyers. I met a few cats from Miami a couple of days ago. The nigga hit my line today discussing prices. He's willing to okay seventeen a key. According to him, Jacksonville still taxing twenty-five a block," Sincere added.

"That's sweet. What's the hold-up?"

"The nigga wants us to deliver the shit personally."

"That depends on what he's spending. If he ain't buying over ten we ain't moving nowhere." Tipton accepted the blunt from Chocolate's hand.

"Smooth, that's a hundred and seventy grand every play. I'll lick a fat girl ass for that much paper in one day?" Rex choked on the weed.

"Remind me not to smoke behind yo' ass again." Sincere laughed.

"You really think we can trust a person we don't know buying over ten?" Chocolate asked.

"It doesn't matter, once he gets down there, he'll pick the location and make them come to him. Our dope, our rules. Besides, they ain't gonna want no part of who I'm sending down there with you."

"Since you put it like that, I'ma go ahead and put that in play, right now." Sincere walked out of the kitchen.

"Well, if you all will excuse me, I got a date this morning with a lil' freak-a-leek. She finna drop down and get her eagle on with this nutsack." Rex flipped the collar on his shirt. "Say, Chris Brown, I'ma bring that paper to ya spot after I finish up." He slapped Tipton on the back before leaving.

"I think Rex's mama dropped him on his head," Chocolate huffed.

"Hmm, I think it was his neck."

"So, you serious about me teaching Meisha and them the recipe?" She asked with a hand on her chin.

"Yeah, that don't mean show them how to bring back a whole chicken. Show them the basics and see if they catch on. If not, let they ass continue to be a bag up girl."

Chocolate stared at him and tilted her head. "Tip, you haven't even taught me how to perfect it. Yet, I been messing up all types of four ways and nines."

"But you got the blueprint and you're my top lady. You know I got you."

"I wish I was yo' top lady." She rubbed a hand through his waves.

"You know I got mad love for you girl, don't do that."

"Maybe if you would've listened to me about that slime ass bitch, Peaches, I could've been your baby mama."

"We all make mistakes, Chocolate. Before I went to prison, I was young, still immature to certain things and just couldn't understand what real was."

"I'm still in love with you." She gazed in his eyes. "I know I shouldn't be."

Taking a deep breath, he grabbed her hand. "Look, no matter what happens with our business, we will always remain friends. I will never turn my back on you period. You're like a sister to me."

Chocolate shook her head, then leaned over and pecked his lips before he could reject. "Thanks, but that's not enough for me." She stood out of her chair and exited the kitchen.

Thinking to himself, Tipton realized it would never be enough love to go around. Everyone had a different objective while he was only focused on one thing. Taking the game for it all.

****

Northside Rehabilitation Center

After Tipton made his way into the building of Lisa's drug facility, the nurse smiled as he came forward to the counter. "Hi, Mr. White, sign in for me and I'll take you back to her."

"Sure." He grabbed the clipboard and pen.

She placed it back down and led him to the lounge where the patients spent their day. "She's been very agitated lately. Hopefully, seeing you can cheer her up a bit?" She pointed at Lisa sitting in front of a television.

Tipton nodded and made his way over to her. As he moved through the tight area, he stepped behind her chair. "How are you?"

Lisa looked up into his face, jumped from her seat and latched onto his neck. "Tip, is it time for me to go home now?"

Tipton knew he couldn't lie, so he cleared his throat and broke the news to her. "Not yet, it's only been two days. I need to make sure these doctors help you in every way before I bring you home."

"Help me! I been sitting here watching Titanic for thirty-six hours straight and that white bitch keep asking me all these crazy ass questions. You ain't helping nothing by leaving me here," she ranted.

"First off, stop yelling and calm down. Secondly, you have to understand, I'm doing what's best for you. I refuse to let you go out bad in them streets."

"So, now you're a fucking mind reader? Tell me what's gonna happen then bitch, huh?"

"You're gonna get worse using that drug and you'll eventually overdose and die."

Lisa clapped loudly in his face and started pulling off all her clothes. "I ain't dead yet. How can you deny me the same shit, you selling motherfucker? You think I don't know? You just like yo' evil ass mama."

"Listen, stop that shit!" Tipton tried to calm her down, as she stripped in front of all the patients.

As the two nurses ran in to restrain her, Lisa began to get belligerent. "Oh, what y'all here to rape me? I'ma need some motherfucking co-pay if you thinking about touching this dope head pussy. Take me home! Take me home!" She screamed.

Looking on in disbelief, Tipton placed a hand on his face as the head doctor approached him. "Maybe she just needs a little time alone to find herself. I'll be sure to give you a call if things get better."

"Thank you," Tipton replied, before making his way out of the center.

It was hard to see a close friend of the family going through a serious tribulation. Struggles with others would always be a main distraction. Whether physically or mentally. All he could do was stand firm until he climbed his way to the top.

Chapter 16

Tipton slid up to Peaches crib and stepped out of his car after replying to Chocolate's text message. He knocked on the door, it opened seconds later with Kimmi stepping out first.

"Hey, baby." He smiled embracing her.

As he looked up at Peaches who stood in the doorway, he balled up his face. Her eye was swollen black. "What the fuck happened to you?"

She was shuffling the cigarette in her hand, she smacked her teeth before sparking it. "You happened to me. I guess you've just gotten to the point where you don't wanna fuck wit' me at all."

"I said what happened to your face?" his voice grew louder.

"Wouldn't you like to know? It was just a small catfight. Nothing I can't handle. Maybe if you get back with me, I can have my family back and shit wouldn't occur."

"I tried that and unfortunately, I got the shitty end of the stick."

"I'm asking for one last chance," she said on the verge of tears, as her hands trembled.

Observing her movements and words, Tipton could sense that something else was wrong with her. "Look, we've been through tons of shit that can never be taken back. Our minds are on two different levels when it comes to bonding with each other. Kimmi is our main focus, regardless of issues and attitudes. If you need anything, then you can get it. But we just don't have time to reheal this broken problem." Tipton didn't want to hurt her feelings.

"I'm going through a lot, Tipton. My heart is aching and I'm about to crack," she mouthed, as a tear dropped from her left eye. "Nobody's perfect and I know I might have said some crazy things, but don't turn your back on me now. Please!"

Only if his eyes could see Dejuan on the other side of her door with a pistol to her head, his heart would've made an exception. "I'll talk to you in a few days, Peaches." He walked off.

As she lowered her head, Peaches received a hard slap to the face. "Sound like you was trying to give that fuck nigga a clue about me? Get yo' ass up!" Dejuan yelled with spit flying from his mouth.

Shaking like a leaf, Peaches stood to her feet. Dejuan grabbed her by the hair and pushed her towards the bedroom. He opened the door with his foot, then pushed her back inside.

He unbuckled his belt, letting his pants fall to the floor. "Get over here and take that shit off."

Peaches slid her shorts and panties from her body as she stared in fear. Seeing her goods pushed him to the edge. He quickly bent her over the bed in aggression causing Peaches to scream.

****

After stopping by the new constructed park in the area, Tipton decided to share a meal with his pride and joy. He couldn't help but smirk at his little one while she poured the mountain dew inside her small cup.

"Daddy?" She sat the twenty-ounce bottle on the table.

"Waddup pumpkin?"

"I don't like that man."

"What man, Kimmi?" Tipton was confused.

"The man at mommy house." She bit into her cookie.

"Your mama be having a man over there with you in the house?"

"Yes, he's mean to me."

Hearing her words caused even more disgust for Peaches in his heart. She truly had the nerve to speak about having a family when she was indulging with another man in front of their seed.

It was definitely a problem that would be confronted the next time she crossed his path.

****

Saturday Afternoon

After Rex came to scoop Kimmi the next morning, Tipton and Halo made their way past Lindbergh transit heading for Atlantic station. As they pulled through the streets of the huge shopping area, Tipton turned inside the movie theater and shut off his engine.

"Same thing, bro. Keep your eyes open. Hopefully, I shouldn't be too long."

"Already, God."

Tipton climbed out of the rented S.U.V, then spotted Rika standing in front of the entrance with a smile across her face. Her sexy top nearly exposed most of her cleavage and the tights she wore cuffed every part of her model-like body.

"Hey, Tipton," she mouthed before hugging him. She buried her pretty face into his chest, inhaled his *Polo* black cologne and instantly became aroused.

"Waddup, Rika?" He placed a kiss on her cheek.

"The same as usual, I got us two tickets to this romantic movie to pass a quick twenty minutes. We have to catch the last of it." She pulled his hand to head inside.

"You bought tickets for a movie that's about to end. What was the point of that?" Tipton asked.

"Because if you've ever been to the movies for a love flick you would know that the best parts are always at the end," she mentioned before handing the rope man their passes.

Heading through the dark movie room, they moved up the steps until finding a section far in the back. "I thought we were supposed to be handling business, Rika? You never told me that enjoying a romance was in the equation."

"This is business. Besides, the next time we meet you'll be speaking to him directly." She leaned her head against his shoulder.

Smiling at her persistence and unique structure, Tipton sat back and relaxed. As the last five minutes of the movie crept around, Rika's womanhood started to tingle from the erotic scene that played on the screen.

"I guess you were right, the end of a romantic is crazy," Tipton whispered still tuned in.

Feeling the rush in her body, she couldn't contain herself. She unzipped Tipton's jeans, grabbed ahold of his piece and released it from the boxers.

"Yo' Rika, what the fuck?"

She wrapped her small lips around his member, Rika sucked as if her life depended on it. "Shit," Tipton mumbled while looking down at her.

As she opened her mouth wider, saliva dribbled from the corners of her lips. Rika took more of him down and started bobbing her head at a rabbit's pace, she placed Tipton's hand between her legs to caress her throbbing clit. By the time the movie was ending, Tipton was shooting his load into her mouth. He leaned back in satisfaction.

He grabbed the back of her head, Rika continued to down him until swallowing everything he offered. After Rika adjusted his jeans, she looked into his brown eyes.

"We can go now, big man."

Her seductive behavior always put him in a perplexed situation. On the same note, her freakiness is what kept him amorously attracted to her. Even though he knew it wasn't right, Rika seemed like an expert with catching him off guard.

As they walked out of the movie theater, Rika hugged his waistline and put the address for their next meet in his palm. "You doubled your supply? I take it that things are going well?"

"Better than I imagined. I'm putting some power pieces in effect to expand a little more. You only limited to how far you push yourself," he said his mind still elsewhere.

Straightening the wrinkles in his shirt, she kissed his neck. "Your last name is, White. There's no such thing as limit in your vocabulary. I'll be waiting on your call."

Watching her strut away, Tipton replayed her remark back through his head. When he thought about it, she was right. Taking chances with the penitentiary would be the same whether he purchased large or small quantities. There was no more reasons to half step.

Tipton climbed back inside the car. As he glanced at the packages in the backseat, he tapped Halo. "Who was it?"

"The same two girls it was the first time, God. They acted like I wasn't even sitting in the front seat. They grabbed the money, put the work in the back and left."

Tipton really couldn't put his hand on it, but he knew that Rika was smarter than she seemed. Her drop-offs were so secretive you wouldn't even know when the shipment was delivered.

"I'm sending you to handle that with Sincere tomorrow. I haven't done too much homework on these Florida cats, but they talking about grabbing twelve of them. Now Sincere might be good on the business, but that don't mean he got an eye to spot any fuck shit. If it goes well, take you seventeen off the top. Any sideways action, dirt nap everybody," Tipton ordered.

"However, you feel God."

If his connections were granted in the streets of Miami, it would be the ticket that separated the small league from the major bosses.

Chris Green

Chapter 17

As Tipton stepped out of the bathroom, he sprayed himself with the *Gucci* Cologne from his dresser. Then he scanned his appearance in the mirror, his button-down sleeves were rolled up to the elbow. His black slacks matched the black *Louis Vuitton* slippers and his haircut was fresher than usual. He made his downstairs as he brushed his hair.

"Damn, Prince Harry, where the hell you off to?" Rex asked while sitting at the table. He was breaking down a pound of marijuana.

Tipton tossed a piece of gum in his mouth and smiled.

"Oh, you about to go and get you a piece of that Barbie doll, huh?"

Tipton laughed as he took a seat on the couch. "Nah, not yet. We gon' slide over to the Cheesecake Factory and snatch something to eat. Afterward, we might go and do a little paint session down on Peachtree."

"*Paint*, nigga when you gon' paint them big ass buns she toting in them pants? Shawty got one of them sexual seduction booties," Rex remarked and nodded like *Snoop Dogg*.

"Watch ya mouth 'bout that one." Tipton chuckled.

Rex broke down a cigar, quickly filled it to the max and rolled it to perfection. "So, you think lil' mama might be the one this time? I don't need you pulling no *O.J. Simpson* if shit ain't working out the way you want."

"You, stupid man. I feel Nita is perfect for me. Her vibe is just so different. She's smart and she knows what she wants out of life. You ain't gon' find too many twenty-four-year-old women who are college-educated and snatching up a degree for a real career. I'm definitely ready to pop that question on shorty." Tipton pictured her in a gorgeous wedding gown.

"If you thinking about putting a ring on her finger, she gon' hate me. I'm throwing a bachelor party and it ain't nothing walking through the door but some midget strippers." Rex nodded while pulling on the blunt.

"Remind me not to invite yo' crazy ass." Tipton headed for the door.

"When Kimmi wakes up, I'ma go take her to grab something to eat."

"Cool, I'll be back in a few hours."

"Smooth." Rex placed his attention back on the table.

Tipton jumped into his flashy whip, started the ignition and pulled off.

****

Cheesecake Factory

East Point, GA

After enjoying a wonderful lunch with Nita, Tipton sat at the table staring at her while waiting for their dessert to be delivered.

"Whattt?" She grinned with a shy expression.

"I'm just thinking, I can't help but do that when I'm around you."

"About what?"

"Everything, life, prospering and love."

As the waitress sat Nita's double chocolate cake on the table, Tipton handed her a fifty-dollar bill.

"You gave her fifty bucks just for dropping off a piece of cake. I would be happy to wait your table."

Tipton picked up the fork and put a piece to her lips. Nita smiled as she put her mouth around the silverware tasting the rich flavor. "Money is just used to take care of basic needs, Nita. I would love to pamper you even more."

"You're too good to me." She slid closer to him.

"I want to be great for you. In this world, you got two types of people. The ones who lie and the ones that prove. Taking the time to build a relationship is like a card house. One false move and you could ruin it all. I refuse to let that happen with me and you."

"A normal life will suffice for me, Tipton. It's the time that makes the joy remarkable in my heart."

"Come on, I wanna show you something." He stood up and held out his hand. After leading her out of the Cheesecake factory, they got in the car and headed straight for Peachtree Street.

****

Tipton slipped his car into the parking deck, then he and Nita walked two blocks down the road until he stopped in front of a medium-sized building. They entered through the glass doors and wandered inside the huge white studio. Plastic was placed gently on the floor with tons of painting utensils and different frames and paper leaked against the wall ready for use.

"I was thinking we could have one more challenge in a real painting studio where I can be more comfortable." Tipton adjusted the sleeves on his shirt.

"You're on." She took off running towards a certain paintbrush she spotted.

After jumping into action for the first ten minutes, Tipton sat his painting pen down. "I'm not even finna sit here and embarrass myself like this. You, win."

"Don't get scared now. I haven't even got all the way into my picture yet."

He wrapped his hand around her waist and smooched her passionately. I can't beat you in something you've already won, baby."

"Oh, yeah. What do I win then?" she asked in a gentle tone.

"All of this," he said looking around the studio.

"What?"

"I figured you needed the space. Not only will your buyers see your work on the internet. They can come to view it in your own shop."

"This is mine?" she asked in disbelief.

Tipton held up the key for the front entrance. "Yep."

Screaming with excitement, Nita jumped into his arms planting numerous kisses on him. "Thank you! Thank you! This will help me pay off my tuition, Tipton."

"I paid off your tuition last week, ma, stop stressing that."

Knowing that she had to be the luckiest girl ever, Nita smiled and hugged his neck tightly. "I love you!"

"I love you, too, beautiful."

Tipton rubbed on her slim waist and studied her with a slight grin. "You can look at my picture now if you want to."

"What did you do this time, another stick figure?" She stepped in front of his board. Staring at the words, *Will you marry me?* Made Nita gasp, as she turned to face him. "Are you serious, Tipton?"

She watched him remove a small ring box and get down on one knee. Then she covered her mouth and began to tremble.

"Nothing else has made me happier these few months except meeting a queen like you. I don't need to second guess or ask myself can I wake up to you every morning. Sex isn't important. Neither do I care about others having an opinion on my decision. I truly love you and even though it's only been a few months. I feel like we could plan a gorgeous wedding in a few months. I just want you. Will you marry me?" he asked with a cheesy ass smile.

As the tears flushed down her cheek, Nita nodded and walked over to him. Tipton slid the expensive diamond on her finger, then stood to his feet and placed another kiss on her forehead.

"I love you, Mrs. White," he said with a secure hug.

"I love you, too, baby," she whispered as the tears fell down his shirt.

Chapter 18

Sincere and Halo sat in the tiny hotel room, waiting patiently for the new Miami clientele to arrive. Time was starting to tick, and they began to feel that the purchase was a dummy mission. Two hundred grand was something they definitely didn't want to risk for a guy who was talking a good game.

Peeping the Denali Yukon truck pull inside of the lot, Sincere watched as the man climbed out of the truck with his associates.

"They here," Sincere alerted Halo, who was posted against the wall.

Nodding his head in silence, Halo pulled out his twin 9mm handguns letting them dangle by his side. Before the men could knock, Sincere opened the door allowing them to enter.

"Gentlemen, it's a pleasure to see you, but you're late," he addressed when they crossed the threshold.

"You fellas will have to excuse my absence. Something came up, but all is well. This is who I wanted you to meet," the Miami connect said, as a Spanish man stepped forward.

"The name is, Kenny Quick, bro." He held out his hand.

His black hair was smoothed to the back and his entire mouth was glistening with gold. His collar shirt was unbuttoned at the top exposing the taco meat that rested on his chest and his appearance was something straight out of the seventies.

"It's nice to meet you, but if you don't mind, I would like to count this money so we can complete the business." Sincere pointed towards the money counter.

"I think you'll see that my business is always correct. I would like to see the product, my man."

As Halo gripped his pistols, he gazed at Kenny with a funny eye. Tossing a kilo from the bag, Sincere watched as he punctured the center lightly with a razor, tasting a sample of the product, then he smiled.

"A pure white freak!" he shouted while nodding to his worker.

After sitting the bag on the floor next to Sincere, the brawny bodyguard opened it. After the funds were sent through the machine and counted correctly, Sincere looked at Halo. "It's all here."

Halo placed the duffle bag of drugs on the floor and used his foot to push it towards Kenny.

"I think this is gonna be the start of a wonderful friendship. Hopefully, we can meet within the next few weeks. I don't know if you boys are hip to the Florida life? But prices like these don't come around often. It was surely a pleasure." He flashed a crooked smile while shaking Sincere's hand.

"I wouldn't care if you wanted it every week. As long as the money is being spent, we have business."

"Sounds good, next time guys."

Halo watched the strange man exit out of the door, he stared until they climbed back into the truck to leave. "None of that seemed weird to you, God?" Halo tossed the bag of money around his back.

"What do you mean?" Sincere seemed puzzled.

"I don't know, he just seemed too eager."

"He just wants to sound like a boss with all that fake ass Puerto Rican, Johnny shit. I'm used to meeting clowns like him, trust me. That's the reason I keep the small talk short and get the bread. Let's just get the hell out of here so we can make this long ass drive back," Sincere replied before they exited the room.

They returned the room key, then headed back to Atlanta with a new clientele that was about to show them exactly why Miami was the distribution capital.

****

6:30 p.m.

After Tipton pulled away from Spelman College campus, he stared in his rearview, as Nita made her way inside the University for her Night Accountant Classes. It was amazing how he could share so much with a friend that was now his fiancée. Treasure was supposed to be hard to come across, but Tipton's had landed right in his lap. Everything fell exactly as he pictured and now that he'd popped the hard question, it was time to start planning his future.

He felt his phone vibrating and picked it up. "Waddup, bro?"

"Tip, we got a problem it's, Peaches," Rex said with worry.

Hearing his baby mother's name made him sigh in disappointment. "What the fuck did she do now?"

"She's in the hospital, I found her beat up pretty bad on the bedroom floor."

"What?"

"Yeah, me and Kimmi are down at South Side Medical."

"I'm on my way." He hung up.

Tipton made a sharp u-turn in the middle of the street, headed for the expressway. He smashed into the hospital parking lot, got out of his car and speeded through the emergency room entrance.

He saw Rex and his daughter posted by Peaches' door and moved towards them. "How bad is it?"

"It ain't good, but she's awake," Rex replied.

Tipton peeped through the small window, made his way inside and gazed at her hideous, swollen jaw and battered black eye, shaking his head.

"Tip," she cried looking over at him.

"What happened, Peaches?" he uttered moving closer to her.

Tears poured down her beaten face, Peaches opened her mouth to speak, "I don't want you to be mad at me."

"What the fuck are you talking about? Who did this to you? What are you trying to hide so bad, Peaches?" He folded his arms.

"Juan." She closed her eyes.

"What!" Tipton's rage began to rise when his name escaped her mouth. He also wasn't blind from the betrayal of her sheer behavior. Word of her and Dejuan creeping was thrown up in the air from some private associates on numerous occasions. It was a complete disgust in his mind and he still hadn't gotten the chance to clarify the suspicious activities between them. "Peaches, I'm gonna ask you one time and one time only. Have you been fucking this nigga behind my back?" He rubbed his temple to relax a bit.

Her fingers shuffled with nervousness. "Baby, he hurt me," she tried to devise an excuse.

"Answer the damn question and quit bullshitting me shawty!"

"It was never anything serious," she whispered.

Staring at her with a vexed expression, Tipton stepped closer to her. "Out of every man you picked to sleep with! You chose a nigga who's supposed to be my potna?"

"I didn't want to hurt you."

"You ruined our family. You deceived me when I was at my lowest. Make sure when that nigga kills yo' ass he got enough money to bury you, bitch!" Tipton spat before leaving out of the room.

Tipton watched Rex lower his gaze and chuckled. "You knew, didn't you?"

"Bro, it wasn't my place to speak on—"

"Nigga, you supposed to be my fucking friend! The slime ass boy been waxing my baby mama and you ain't even put me on game not once." Tipton gave him a look laced with disgust.

"Hold up fool, I warned you that girl wasn't shit while you was behind the wall. Neither was that dirty ass nigga, Dejuan. You never listened to the signs, Tip. I can only say so much," Rex said truthfully.

"All you had to do was speak, nigga. We been friends since I was thirteen, Rex. It's certain things that you just don't let slide when you say that you truly fuck with me, bro. Let's go, Kimmi." He grabbed his daughter's hand.

"Tip, you my dawg, bro. I don't ever want you to feel like I'm your enemy. Don't make me feel that way, straight up," Rex warned.

"Yeah, whatever, I'll holla at you later my nigga. I need to take my daughter home." He ignored his remark and left the hospital.

It was evident that Rex was his friend, but there was still a line of disloyalty that was never supposed to be crossed. Still in all, no love was lost. From now on, it was only gonna be strictly business, friends or not.

Chris Green

Chapter 19

Sliding his whip inside of Deerfield's garden, Juan parked directly in front of Skeet and his crew who posted on the corner sidewalk.

"You must be lost? This a long way from home," Skeet said as he stepped out of the car.

Recognizing the frowns plastered on all his goons face, Juan knew his reason for showing up would have to be stated quickly. "Nah, I ain't lost, I come in peace. I'm here to scream at you about something."

"Start screaming then, nigga. Your team ain't welcomed on this side of the turf. I don't know if you heard or not, but yo' boy touched the wrong group of niggas. If we ain't receiving no blood and bodies, we ain't got nothing to talk about." Skeet spit on the hood of Dejaun's car.

Knowing that he had to contain his anger, Juan brushed off the disrespectful action. "I'm alone where I'm standing. Whatever those pussy ass niggas got coming for them is a problem they gotta deal with. What does it take for me to be, Louie Gang?" Dejaun asked.

"Oooohhh, I guess you finally came to yo' senses? That sucka been treating you like a pet, huh?"

"Maybe you got me confused with Rex or some shit? I ain't no niggas pet and I'm damn sho' nobody's worker. Neither will I settle for being around niggas with hoe ass intentions. Why do you think I'm standing in front of you, right now?"

Skeet laughed and put both hands in his pockets. Seeing that Dejaun was serious, he took a step forward. "Louie accepts nothing but blood. Anybody can say they wanna eat with this team, but that doesn't mean it's easy."

"I'm still waiting for you to answer the question." Dejaun was unfazed by his statement.

"That pussy drawed blood from our circle. In order to prove loyalty to this side, we need a life that's dear to him, an even swap, no swindle. Does that answer what the fuck you need to know?"

Thinking hard, Dejuan opened his car door, then looked back to Skeet. "I'll be back in three days." He got in his whip and pulled away.

Smiling with a devilish grin, Tipton's face popped into Skeet's head. The time for payback was long overdue. The game of chess was in effect and there could only be one winner.

****

After Chocolate stopped by Tipton's spot for her re-up, he sat at his wide kitchen table counting his earnings by hand.

"So, what are you gonna do about this clown? I think dude pushed too far this time," Sincere stated.

"That boy's time is coming. He don't realize how deep he's digging that hole until it fucks around and cave in on his ass. Peaches got herself in this situation, so I refuse to concern myself with any of that nonsense. I want his head just for the disrespectful shit he's doing."

"True, In due time it'll all play out, bro. We winning right now, all the keys is set up for us to use. Before you know it, that boy will be a mystery. But anyway, my sister told me the good news. Congratulations, my guy. She deserves a good one like you, so I agree. I would hate it if you had to revert to some bullshit because of that duck. Niggas wanna see you back in prison."

"Prison isn't an option for me anymore," Tipton replied. "I love your sister and I ain't breaking my promise for anything or anyone. Wassup with this Miami cat? Is he trying to start copping from us or was it a one-time thing?"

"Listen, that man is about his business. After he tasted how potent yo' shit is, I knew he was on board," Sincere confirmed.

"I don't like that nigga, God," Halo butted in. "I can smell a snake a mile away."

"That's normal, bro. I don't ever want you to like anyone. There's never no telling when we need to get rid of him. So, keep those feelings toward him all the time. But for now, he's spending money so he get a pass." Tipton tossed Halo his cut of the deal.

"Already, God."

After handing Sincere his split, he began bagging the rest of his profits. "If you need more product to hustle, Chocolate will cover it. I need to head upstairs and put this up." He got up from the table leaving them alone.

****

"Damn, that's crazy fam. At the end of the day, you can't babysit the boy. It's not your problem if his bitch running around with loose legs," his young worker said, as Rex played the blackjack machine in the corner store.

"I'll never babysit anyone. Homie or family, I just try to keep it smooth because I'm a real one. I got my own movement out here in these streets. It's starting to die while I'm helping another nigga's status rise. I just wanna get some paper." Rex pulled on the swisher sweet.

"Well, stop playing games and let's focus on booming this gas. You should still have enough supply from the last move you pulled."

"I don't know what you talking about. Stop saying crazy shit in public. Niggas in the hood got ears like, Dumbo. Plus, I got patience, I'll know when my job is done."

"True."

"What time is it?" Rex asked.

"It's eleven 'o clock. What the hook gon' be? You ready to slide out or what?"

Rex stretched his arms, got up and headed for the door. He paused in shock spotting Skeet and two of his men sitting on his car.

"I don't think you comprehend when I said you shouldn't be on the Southside. Or maybe you just don't care." He stared at Rex.

"We just sliding through like grease and making our way back out. Ain't nothing wrong with that, right?"

Rex's mind thought about his strap that rested underneath his car seat. All he could do was hope things didn't lead to a hostile encounter.

Skeet's gunman wasted no time bearing down on them with their guns drawn. "You musta forgot about our last run in? Or shall I say forgot about what you did to my soldiers?" He stepped closer to Rex.

"I don't know what you're talking about, bro?"

"Y'all never do." He nodded for his men to handle the business.

Delivering a shrewd fist to Skeet's eye, Rex made a run for it. He dashed out of the parking lot as bullets from numerous weapons started firing.

Boc! Boc! Boc! Boc!

His worker was quickly put to rest with a slug entering the back of his head. Regaining himself, Skeet took off directly behind him.

Boc! Boc! Boc!

Rex covered his head as the bullets flew past his ears. His heart pounded profusely. He was running for his life.

"I'ma kill you, fuck nigga!" Skeet yelled, as his gun continued to bark.

Boc! Boc!

As Rex ran through the intersecting street, he was nearly blindsided by a speeding car. His feet continued to beat the pavement until he spotted the black truck swerving behind him. The headlights shined brightly, as their weapons erupted with a mission. Noticing a set of woods to his left, Rex sprung into action and made his way through the thick trees. The large branch that caught his foot forced him to trip and hit his face violently on the ground.

Hearing the tires screech to halt, Rex shook off the slip and scurried to his feet. Moving past the slippery molded rocks and deep mud, he placed his back against a large tree. He could feel the thick blood leaking from his forehead, as he tried to settle his erratic breathing. The distant sirens that rang in the background was like music to his ears.

"Skeet, fuck that nigga. We gotta go!" One of the men screamed.

Still holding his position, Rex relaxed after hearing the truck speed away. Making sure the coast was clear, he slowly walked deeper into the woods until he came out behind a small home. Stepping out into the streetlight, he wiped the blood from his face and called Tipton.

Chapter 20

"They caught me down bad and killed my worker. My burner was in the car under the fucking seat. I couldn't do shit else but run," Rex admitted sitting back on the couch.

Tipton shook his head, as he stared at the huge gash on his face. "We gotta get rid of that nigga. We can't focus on getting no bread if this bitch ass nigga around here pulling that lil' boy shit. You just gotta lay low here until you relocate with your spot. The Southside ain't gonna work if you're bumping into this lame on every corner."

"I hear ya. My whip is still parked in front of the damn store. The cops are probably all over my shit by now. I ain't got time to be getting investigated 'bout no murder," he stressed.

"Right now, you can only be grateful that you still have a soul in your body. We can send somebody through there later to pick up yo' shit if it's still there."

"Smooth." Rex sat back and sparked him one.

Tipton walked over to Halo, who sat quietly at the kitchen table, Tipton looked into his blue eyes. "I got you, twenty-five grand a piece for every Louie Gang nigga you rock to sleep. Leave the head honcho for me."

"Whatever you say, God."

****

7:30 a.m.

Dejaun pushed his whip through the Southside streets, he nearly slammed on his brakes after spotting Lisa who roamed around the rehabilitation center's parking lot. Judging from the way she mumbled to herself, he could tell she needed a fix. Noticing that his surroundings were clear, he pulled directly next to her.

"Yo' Lisa?"

Lisa turned her neck faster than an owl and squinted her eyes walking toward him. "Juan, is that you?"

"Shhhh, you ain't gotta scream my name. Why the fuck you sitting at the center? You turning your back or what?"

"You made my nephew flip on me and put me in this crazy home. This yo' fault motherfucker," she cursed with an attitude.

"Fuck, Tipton! You a grown-ass woman. If you wanna get high Lisa, you can. It ain't nothing wrong with doing you. Stop acting brand new. Ain't I been taking care of you?" he said, gripping his dick.

"I don't know why you grabbing that. You fucked up yo' chance to get any more of this." She dropped it low to the ground before standing back up.

"How about I take you to the house and you tighten me up for a nice piece?" He pulled out a small bag of dope.

As he watched her stare at the sack, Juan knew she was weighing her options. She jumped in the front seat and he smirked before pulling out the lot. There was always two sides to the game. He just hoped Tipton could run when the rabbit had the gun.

****

Jackson pulled his Porsche through his nephew's driveway, stepped out and headed for the house. He rang the doorbell, Halo answered and stepped to the side so he could enter.

"What's good with you, baby boy?" He looked at Tipton.

"Waddup?" His tone was dry.

"You mind if I holla at you in private outback?"

Halo's eyes scanned him to see if he spotted a weapon before Tipton agreed to his request. Tipton stood up and moved to the patio door. He allowed Jackson to walk out first and followed.

"Check it out, your pops is a little drunk off y'all last encounter. Even this is hard for him to understand. I explained that certain feelings will probably never be erased because of y'all critical circumstances. He said if you're willing to work with him, you can take charge and the profits will be split fifty-fifty."

"What is it with you and this nigga? I clearly told you the last time I saw this man, that I don't want no dealings with the clown. It's like you're working with him or something?" Tipton ranted, now beyond pissed.

"You are so obnoxious, nephew. I'm in it to see you win. I'm the same one who made sure you were laced when you got home. Remember?"

"Hold the fuck on! Let's get this shit straight, right now. This is my mama's shit. That's paper she left me that was in your possession. Where the fuck is the rest of it? I damn sho' know for a fact that it was supposed to be more than five hundred grand. It's a lot of sneaky ass movements going unanswered. So, before you try to say you made sure I was laced, make sure you put my mama's name in front of that shit when you speak."

Jackson folded his arms and started laughing. "I guess you really smelling yo' motherfucking nuts now, nigga? I set you up with major moves to build your status. This is the type of respect you show me? I'ma let you in on a little secret nephew. It's real wolves out here in the game. Niggas shed blood and put in good work to hold a position in these streets. Competition never lasts long, especially when you think you're too good to let another nigga eat. Vel, is the wrong one to do that with."

"That sounds like a threat. I tell you what, fuck that nigga and fuck you, too."

After hearing the commotion, Halo stepped through the glass door with his pistol in hand. Rex followed closely behind him. "Is there a problem, God?"

Jackson now feeling the young killer's aura, knew that his presence was unwanted.

"Nah, no problem. He was just leaving." Tipton gave him a stern look.

Jackson heeded his warning, turned around and walked out of the back yard.

"He don't look too happy," Rex said walking over to Tip.

"Don't matter, it's time to start buckling down. If you ain't working with us, that means you're our enemy. No exceptions for anyone." He made his way back into the house.

****

After Lisa and Dejaun entered her junked out home, Dejuan locked the door behind him. "I ain't giving up no pussy until I get my co-pay motherfucker. You not gon' trick me like you used to, my nigga."

Dejaun grabbed the poison out of his pocket and placed it in her hand. "I ain't got no reason to flex you, bitch."

Securing her high, Lisa pulled down her pants and bent over the couch. Dejaun rubbed his hand across her slit and smelled the horrible scent that trailed off his fingers.

"How about you just give me some head." He changed his mind.

"Make up yo' mind motherfucker. This ain't no average pussy," she complained and got on her knees.

Ignoring her stupid comment, Juan grabbed the back of her head. Her cold wet lips bobbed up and down, as he humped into her mouth. The choking sounds enticed him even more, as he watched Lisa take his entire length without budging. It didn't take long for him to gather his reckless plan, as he continued to violate her.

Catching his nut, he shot every drop down her throat while grunting in satisfaction. "Nothing extra nigga. Since you passed the chance up with hitting this again." Lisa pulled her pants up.

As Lisa turned her back and reached into her bra, pulling out the packaged drug, this gave Dejuan enough time to unplug the small metal lamp that sat on the side of her couch. He lifted it up high and crashed it down across her skull. Then he watched her crumble to the floor, groaning in pain.

Seeing that the first blow didn't complete the job, Dejuan started hitting her repeatedly.

Whamp! Whamp! Whamp! Whamp! Whamp!

A pool of blood began to form under her head, as she defecated in her pants. Her tense body began to relax, as the last ounce of life escaped her chest. Dejuan dropped the weapon, he stared around the living room. Hoping the flurried disturbance wasn't heard, he quickly dragged her body to the kitchen. He opened the cabinet under the sink, removed the cleaning appliances and grabbed a trash bag. He moved swiftly about cleaning his tracks. Then he snapped a picture of her body and headed out the front door.

Chris Green

Chapter 21

Once he took the trip back to Deerfield Gardens, Juan drove around the parking lot until he found Skeet's truck. He parked, got out the driver's seat and walked over to him. "The man of the hour. You made it back?"

Dejuan passed him the phone without replying, Skeet stared down at the picture of Lisa's stiff body and smiled. "I see you really interested in this Louie life?"

"As I said, I'm with the team who's winning. I ain't no shadow, so I ain't got time to be left in the background." Dejaun grabbed his phone back.

"Once a nigga takes this route, it ain't no turning back. This shit marked on me because I bleed it with a passion." He flashed the cursive *L* to Juan. "Ain't no family, no friends. It's just us cuz we all we got. Decisions are critical. There's no telling if it might be our last."

Walking closer, Dejaun made eye contact. "I want that nigga's head just as bad as you do. He walks around this bitch thinking he's Superman. That boy crossed the line and didn't handle his deed like a G supposed to. Now it's my turn, I ain't gotta be coached in this shit. I'ma grown ass man, either I'm in or out."

Smiling, Skeet shook his hand and locked fists. "Welcome to the gang, my nigga. Step up to my domain so we can brand yo' shit and make it legal."

Hearing the words, he was so desperately waiting on, Juan followed him inside the upstairs apartment.

****

As he stood on the side of CVS pharmacy, Halo sipped on a hot bottle of water, while watching the two Louie gang members lounge around in front of the low budget liquor store. Judging from their relaxed postures, he knew it could've been a possibility that they were concealing a weapon or two. That problem was irrelevant. He just needed to soil their blood smoothly and quiet.

After watching the police cruiser pull inside the space, Halo concealed himself as the white officer stepped out of his car and began harassing the men. Halo tilted the water up to his mouth and huffed. All he could do was wait for the perfect moment.

Sincere interrupted Tipton and Rex from there conversation and walked inside the house with a huge smile on his face. The phone was planted up to his ear, as he sat down and placed a hand on Tipton's shoulder. "Well, that'll be something, I'll let you all discuss," he said into the receiver before passing the phone.

Looking at him with a curious stare, Tipton grabbed the line. "Waddup, who dis?"

"Kenny Quick's the name, my friend. It's a pleasure to meet you."

"Likewise. What can I do for you?"

"Well, after meeting with your associate a few days ago, our meet and greet was a success. Unfortunately, the purchase I made has caused a great problem."

"Really? It seemed like everything was simple and discreet on my end, bro. Issues are something I don't have so can you share this with me because I'm lost."

"Sure, I placed an order for twelve. After our business was handled, I began to spread the blessings around Miami, as I planned if you catch my drift."

"And?"

"Let's just say that things were so pure that I began to receive phone calls for orders I didn't have. It ended too quickly. I'm a man of business and I don't mind tipping my hat when credit is due. To make things more vivid for you, I need sixty and I mean pronto, big guy" Kenny said.

"Excuse me?" Tipton thought he had to be joking.

"Sixty, I'm gonna fill you in on a little info. You have blessed Florida with something I haven't seen since the late eighties. All ties that I have shared with anyone has officially been severed. You're the main socket, my man. Now tell me how do you like your cash, fifties or hundreds?"

Tipton smiled and stood to his feet. "Franklins of course. I'll need three days and I'll ring your line if that isn't a problem."

"As I said the first time. It's a pleasure meeting you. Patience is a virtue." Quick ended the call.

Rubbing his hands, Tipton looked at Sincere. "We got work to do."

"I take it he spoke your language?"

"I think we might need a bigger team on payroll. Rex, you think the rest of your young ones ready to step up to the big leagues or what?"

"No doubt about it. What you got in mind?" he replied.

"Millions, y'all looking at the new Kings of Miami." Tipton dialed Rika's number on the phone.

"That's all I need to hear."

Nodding his head, he stepped towards the back patio. Tipton walked out into the yard just as her voice came through the receiver.

"Hello?"

"I miss you."

"I miss you, too."

"A hundred."

"I love you soo much."

"I love you too, ma." Tipton exhaled deeply as he hung up. The take-off was finally at his door.

Chapter 22

As Halo's patience began to grow thin, he guzzled down the last of his water and tossed it on the side of a garbage can. As he watched the officer continue on with his day, he spotted the chance and took advantage. He pulled the black machete from his pants and locked his vision on both men before moving calmly around the corner. His humbleness was always the key to completing his mission without failing. His job was never easy, but it damn sure wasn't impossible.

Halo stepped inside the liquor store parking lot, moving smoothly with the knife, as if all was normal, catching one of the hustler's attention. Halo wasted no time sprinting towards them. Before the other man could notice the danger that was hauling down on him, Halo's machete penetrated the center of his chest with full force. As he watched the man's life drain in seconds, he removed the blade and chased down his second victim. The man's baggy pants and slow feet was no match for Halo's pumping energy.

Halo chased him through a narrow pathway, reached out and grabbed the collar of his shirt. He hit the back of his head on the concrete and howled out in pain. Halo stood over him and pulled the .38 snub nose from his pocket.

"Don't kill me, my nigga. I'm just a worker, I don't have anything," he pleaded like a bitch.

Halo kneeled down beside him and stuffed the barrel of the gun in his mouth. "It would be very helpful if you tell me who Skeet works for. And before you lie, I'll try to help you remember." He dug the machete into his leg, then placed a bullet directly behind it.

"Fuckkkk! Oh shit, I'm about to faint dog." He panicked after seeing the blood pour down his pants leg. He shook horribly.

"You ready to talk?" Halo mugged.

"Jackson," he uttered through trembling lips.

Hearing the snake's name run through his ear, Halo shook his head in disappointment. He knew Tipton didn't have a true gift for spotting bad people with sneaky motives. It was the total opposite on his end. He was well-aware of anyone carrying a foul spirit.

"He's the reason you can't make it today. Hopefully, you can forgive me in the afterlife, God?"

Halo placed the gun to the bottom of his chin and pulled the trigger five times.

Boc! Boc! Boc! Boc! Boc!

Halo laid the murder weapon on his chest, stepped over his stiff body and dispersed out of the pathway.

****

Jackson made his way into Vel's office and took a seat until he finished his phone call. "You got some info for me?" he asked tossing the cell on the desk.

"Yeah, your duck ass son is being extra rebellious. I think he knows."

"You said you would be able to make this nigga listen. I told you to explain that this competition thing is bad for everybody's health," Vel replied humbly.

"I did what you said. He ain't hearing that shit. His little team is on the come up and working with you ain't part of his agenda. He's starting to get a little too big for his britches."

"If you gotta wrestle with this nigga to cook this dope. What's the point of even keeping him around? Get rid of him!" Vel yelled with hate in his heart.

Looking at him with a crazy expression, Jackson leaned forward. "Are you crazy? That's my sister's son. That's your fucking kid, nigga."

"Fuck a kid, nigga, I ain't never met this young busta. I come around offering the deal of a lifetime. What he do? You think I built my motherfucking reputation up to let a lil' nigga take my shine and paper. Where the fuck is this nigga, Skeet?

You gotta team running around here doing nothing!" Vel barked.

"I've done everything you've asked me to do. Don't try me like I'm one of these rooty poo street punks, Vel. I'm still that same nigga from back in the day."

Laughing, Vel rose from his seat. "I'ma fill you in on something. We are criminals, our job is simple. It's to be the best at what we do. It's about the team winning. I don't think you're fit to handle that position."

"What the fuck you saying to me?" Jackson snapped.

Vel pulled a black handgun from his pants and whacked him across the head. "You heard what the fuck I said. Your time for working with the organization is ova."

"You, stupid motherfucker. I helped you build this shit after all the slime shit you pulled to do it! How you gon' play me?" Jackson held the gash.

"Well, now you can build yo' way out," Vel replied before pulling the trigger.

Boom!

Watching Jackson slump over in the chair, Vel sat the pistol on his desk and took a deep breath. He heard a sharp knock on the door, then Sonya stepped in slowly with her gun raised.

"New objective, sweetheart. Have the cleaning crew come and get rid of this nigga. We're taking matters into our own hands. If he don't want to work for us, he won't live to spend the money he's making."

One thing was for sure, no man could ever break a true hustler. He was positive that if Tipton's close associates started to drop, his arrogant ways would come to an end. There would be no other way to stop it besides kneeling at Vel's feet. That was a promise that he was sure to make reality.

****

After Tipton pulled into Peaches' grandmother's home, he grabbed Kimmi out of her car seat and headed for the door. Before he could knock, she stepped out on the porch.

"Hey," she greeted with a sad tone.

"Waddup? She's already eaten, so she might sleep for the rest of the night. I'll be through to pick her up in a week or so."

Peaches grabbed their daughter from his arms as she looked at him. "I'm truly sorry for not listening to you. I made some bad choices and I regret them, even more, every day that passes, Tipton." She sniffled. "I can't make it without you. At first, I felt that I could. I thought I could handle life on my own because I knew you would never look at me the same when you got home."

Tipton studied her bruised face, still, he couldn't give pity for her disrespectful actions. Being dishonest and unloyal was the two avenues that sent a person down a road of no return. It was easy to understand. Women would play their cards for two days, two months or even two years in order to achieve what they wanted. Whether it's just for sex or materialistic things. After they lose interest, you go through the small stages of her trying to leave without clearly saying it. She doesn't want to hurt your feelings, but her heart has died for the love you all once shared.

Faking arguments for no apparent reason, staying out night and day, or over their so-called friend's house. Once you bite the bait by slapping the shit out of her, or even state that she can get the fuck on. You then become the blame for why the relationship flushed down shit creek. It was a sad journey that he wasn't willing to go down again.

"Peaches, I have no hard feelings towards you ma. When I first met you, I thought we would be together forever. Instead of me taking my time to learn about you, I rushed to have something that wasn't going to last. I'm sorry about that and I came to the conclusion that we truly have nothing in common. Hopefully, we can co-parent and do our best for, Kimmi."

"Tip, please, I understand that I messed up. I'm asking you to pardon my mistake and give me one last shot? I'm not perfect, but I accept my wrong, I get it, baby."

"I'm getting married, Peaches. I've found someone. I felt that if I told you, it was gonna be a problem. I didn't want to hurt you."

"*Married*! And you think I'ma sit back and watch you do some stupid shit like that to me?" She squinted her eyes evilly.

"You have no choice. This ain't no fucking gimmick girl. I know you can't accept the horrid truth of this matter. But in time you will." Tipton prepared to walk off.

"If you think you're gonna pull some bullshit like that. You might as well blow my fucking brains out bitch! You hear me?" she screamed in a spiteful rage.

"Goodnight, Peaches."

Watching him walk to the car, she eyed him. Foolish thoughts began to fill her head. "If you do this, I'm not going to stop."

Her speech fell on deaf ears, Tipton backed out of the driveway and pulled off.

****

1:30 a.m.

As the rain poured invading the poisoned streets, Tipton sat in his darkroom flipping through the channels on his sixty-inch plasma. The blunt that burned between his lips soothed his lungs as he pondered on the history with Peaches. It was amazing that you could spend a few years away and make it back to society with a different outlook on your own family. His new success in the game was more gas to the fire. No one liked to see another prosper in something they've worked their entire life to achieve. It was all apart of making a name and being the best hustla that a city could witness. You would always suffer when adding friends to business. Turmoil would always creep around you when a hurt woman didn't want to let go. These were issues Tipton knew would eventually come. A feeble soul would be subdued to the treachery, but a strong mind would keep a stern devotion for their objective.

The sound of his doorbell ringing broke his trance, grabbing his Glock 18 handgun from under the pillow, Tipton placed a bullet in the chamber. As he stepped into the hallway, the bell sounded again. He moved slowly down the steps and glanced out of the peephole. After he hurriedly answered the door, she stood in front of him wearing a soaking wet silk dress. Her hair dripped down her back and she wore an unreadable facial expression.

"Nita, are you okay, baby? Talk to me." He caressed the side of her face. She stepped past him into the house, he followed and closed the door behind them. "Baby, it's one-thirty in the morning. Why are you out here like this?"

"I can't sleep, Tipton. I can't stop thinking about you. I had a very bad dream yesterday and I really needed to be around you."

He hugged her neck, then placed a sweet kiss on her temple. Nita smelled so sweet. "I'm here, ma. You ain't gotta go nowhere," he whispered.

"Can you lay down and hold me?"

Tipton grabbed her hand and led her up to his room. They climbed on the bed, and he pulled her next to him. He reached for the remote beside him, clicking the button to power on his flatscreen. The entertainment channel that was airing, played *Musiq SoulChild's* hit song, '*Love*,' at a moderate volume.

Feeling her inhale deeply, she gripped him tightly. Her wet clothes clung to her body. Tipton's mind was jumping in a million places. Every time she was around, butterflies erupted through his stomach. The scent of her hair and her warm smooth skin tickled his nose.

"Tipton?" Juanita uttered.

"Yes, baby?"

"I'm ready."

"Huh?" His mind didn't comprehend at the second.

Rubbing his cheek, she placed her tongue into his mouth with a passionate kiss behind it. "I'm ready," she repeated.

Tipton's heart pumped heavily. Her remark caught him off guard. All he could do was match her seductive gaze. Juanita's eyes sparkled, showing the steamy emotions caged within.

Rising off the bed, she allowed her dress to fall. Staring at her magnificent body caused him to move towards her. Juanita's slim waist complimented her soft legs and perfect butt. Her dark-colored skin glistened. She was drop-dead gorgeous, irresistible. The Paris Hilton perfume on her body floated with the breeze, as he maneuvered his hands down her intoxicating frame.

Their lips met exploring gently, Tipton held her coke bottle hips. He eased her down onto the bed, dropped his clothes and mounted her. The sweet pecks started from the neck and trailed lightly down to her perky C-cup breasts. His tongue caressed her nipples with ease. Moaning in delight, Juanita arched her back, as her fingers roamed through his deep waves, while he continued down to her stomach. Reaching her gorgeous pussy lips, he spread her legs and put his lips to action. Clawing at the soft mattress, she panted.

"Tipton!"

The whisper of his name fueled him even more. His pace increased, as he rubbed, licked and kissed her. Tipton was dedicated to seeing her reach the ultimate satisfaction. Juanita's eyes rolled to the back of her head. The blissful build up erupted from her womanhood like a ticking time bomb. Still pleasing her, Tipton continued to massage her clitoris. He took another seven minutes to taste a round of her sweet juices.

Raising up, he wiped the cum across her thighs before sinking into Nita's slippery walls, she was tight. Her hazel pupils glistened as he stroked at an even rhythm.

"Mmm," she hummed feeling him dig deeper.

Kissing her face, Tipton started to pump slightly faster. The sound of her second orgasm gushing forth grew louder. Twirling her fingers across his six-pack, she watched as his thick rod stretched her tiny hole.

"Are you okay?" He was looking into her beautiful face.

All she could do was stare. Juanita's mouth was wide from the strokes he was delivering. He turned her over, his hand slid down her body until he reached her soft ass. He guided his way inside, her leg trembled from his size. Her ass clapped gently on his dick. Tipton grabbed her waist for leverage.

"I got you baby." He stroked deeper.

Looking over her shoulder, Juanita gazed at his masterpiece sculpting a picture in the pussy. Her pussy spoke louder with every long pump he enforced. As their bodies became one, flashes began to jolt through her brain. His delicate kisses. The feeling in her stomach, as he dug inside. It was unexplainable. She couldn't contain all the orgasms that flooded out of her body. Tipton pleased her using all nine inches. The hard strokes caused her to bite down on her bottom lip. He would always show the kitty some compassion for a second if she began to fidget. It was beyond a night that was special, it was unforgettable. A night to say that she truly loved the man who laid down his passion for her.

Chapter 23

Tipton's heart fluttered as he opened his eyes the next morning, looking at Nita resting peacefully beside him. Her heavenly scent invaded his nostrils. He wrapped his arms around her. As he rubbed up and down her back, she opened her eyes.

"Good morning."

"Waddup, baby?" He kissed her lips and cheeks.

"You."

Tipton's hand ran smoothly across her soft behind. The episode from the night before began to play through his head. Nita was a prize possession. He couldn't understand how anyone could hurt or deny love for a woman that was so sweet and beautiful.

"Can I get you anything to drink?" He rolled out of bed.

"Coffee, baby."

Blowing her a kiss, Tipton headed downstairs. No words could describe how happy he was at the time. It was nothing better than experiencing true feelings for a person who loved hard. It all felt more than right.

Sincere's loud V8 motorep could be heard from inside, as he pulled in Tipton's driveway. Unlocking the front door, his friend stepped out of his whip and crossed the threshold of his home.

"Waddup, why the hell you look so angry my guy?" Tipton slid back in the kitchen.

"Yo' boy Dejuan is wassup. He pulled a strap on me," Sincere replied furiously.

"What, when did this happen?"

"About an hour ago. He's riding around with Skeet and his crew. They stressing this Louie Gang shit now. Wassup with that?"

Staring out of the window in front of him, Tipton began to think. Juan was playing some foul ass games and it was obvious that he wanted to die. He was pushing the limit with the foolery. The problems were starting to become annoying.

"I wanna know who the fuck over these clowns. Somebody got these niggas playing real sour cause I'm sure Skeet ain't calling no fucking shots."

"If we don't do something about him, shit is gonna get real messy. He ain't about to fuck up this paper." Sincere waited for clarification.

Coming down the steps, Halo stepped into the kitchen and took a seat at the table. "We not about to lose out on anything because of, Juan. Don't nobody owe that boy shit. He already showed us what side he's working. What's understood, don't have to be explained. It's time to tighten up on some extra security for this movement. If the opportunity presents itself, I'll let Halo pour that boy's soul out. Call Rex and let him know to meet us at Chocolate's house in the next twenty minutes."

Tipton grabbed a glass mug from the cabinet, fixed Nita's cup of coffee and headed back upstairs. She sat up in the bed once he stepped back through the door. "Is everything okay? I heard Sincere yelling."

"Yeah, he good. It was just a bad conversation with some people he ain't really feeling. You know how that be."

"Yeah." She grabbed the coffee being careful not spill any.

"I'm about to slide out with him for about a cool hour. You can just make yourself at home. Everything you need for a shower is in the bathroom. My house is your house baby, literally." Tipton smooched her lips.

"Are you sure there's nothing wrong?"

"Positive."

Accepting his answer, Juanita watched him grab a jacket from the closet and depart from the room. All Nita could think about was taking Tipton's last name. "Mrs. White," she mumbled to herself.

Her ring was gleaming every time she moved her hand. It felt great. Nothing would be able to prosper from a couple if there wasn't a friendship established. That was a duty he set out to accomplish by any means. Tipton was showing his true dedication to making her wifey. As she daydreamed of her wedding, a smile spread on her face, all was perfect.

****

Sonya opened Vel's office door and peeked her head inside. "They're here."

Lighting the cigar, he stood to his feet with a wry smile. Vel quickly made his way to the front and entered the living room. Skeet, Dejuan and three Louie gang members posted around as if they were in a five-hundred-dollar apartment instead of a million-dollar home.

"Gentlemen, I'm glad to see that you boys could make it. I think it's about time we have a round table discussion about a few things."

"Where the fuck is, Jackson?" One of Skeet's goons asked.

Following the order that was given to her, Sonya pulled the Glock from the center of her back and released a bullet through the man's skull. *Boc!*

The loud bang caused everyone to jump before his body collapsed. "Anybody got any questions?" Vel stared at the last four men.

Looking at Sonya who still pointed her weapon, Dejuan smirked.

"I'll take the silence as no. I'll be very frank and try not to hold you fellas up too long. To my understanding, you, niggas are running around with no structure. I sit in this big chair for a reason, which is why you're standing in front of me now."

Walking over to Skeet, Vel folded his arms. "I hear you're supposed to be the head. Besides offering the little work y'all moving, what else do you have this crew doing? What else do Louie Gang niggas do?"

"I make everybody move in these streets to lay our names in concrete. Ain't no such thing as structure when it comes to stressing the gang," Skeet replied in a strong tone.

"Did Jackson tell you some stupid shit like that? It's always motherfucking structure when you're operating any organization dumb ass lil' boy. Right now, y'all fucking up. It was an order to handle the kid." Vel inhaled on the Maduro.

"What the hell you want us to do? We're trying to put the press down and do this shit quietly as possible. It's still a live beef going on. You want me to just walk up to the nigga's front door and ask him to cook the crack for us. It's kinda hard to do that without having to kill this bitch in the process."

"I thought that y'all was about that type of shit. Using y'all muscle. It shouldn't be that difficult. I don't give a fuck what you gotta do. If that ungrateful bitch wanna keep his life, he'll abide by the rules and play fair. All we need is the recipe."

"I can make it happen," Dejuan challenged.

Turning his attention to him, Vel pointed as if he found his lucky contestant. "What makes you so sure about that statement?"

"Because I know everything about that boy. I'm talking about like the back of my hand. I can get close to him."

"That shit sounds real convincing. I'll tell you what, the first person that can get the instructions on how to flip a bird out of this nigga. I'ma give you a hundred bands of his salary, cash."

"Done," Dejuan agreed hearing the chedda that was offered.

"My man." Vel smiled while shaking his hand.

Cutting his eyes over at Juan, Skeet headed for the door.

"Remember that going against the grain is bad for everybody's health. We don't need no renegade shit in this crew. It's only one job and that's to make him cough up what we need. If he doesn't comply, force him to," Vel commanded before they exited his home.

Looking at Sonya, who stood quietly, he placed a hand on her waist. "Follow them around for a few days. If you can't see any progress, get rid of all of them." Vel watched as she exited the room. A quick thought of Mary popped in his brain. Her son wanted to fall in her exact steps. He wanted to control the entire city so the rest could suffer and eat out of his palm. It was a task that Vel would crash horribly. Even if it meant murdering more flesh and blood.

****

"I told you that county ass boy was no good. He turns around and links up with the same niggas that busted at your squad. He needs to die." Rex had venom flying from his tongue.

"I agree, bro, Juan is leaving a bad taste out there, right now. He running around with all this crazy shit. Pulling dumb ass stunts. What other options are we left with?" Sincere said, with worry eating through his voice.

"First off, this ain't no masked goon who been out here placing people under the dirt. This is Dejuan we talking about. He always been a bitch. That boy can fool everyone else, but not me," Tipton spat.

"Hold up, Tip. I know you don't play, but you musta forgot that you were gone for four years. A lot of shit happened in that small time-frame. That dumb ass nigga was out here shooting everybody he could. We don't need to be sitting here clueless. Ain't no telling what's on Juan's mind." Chocolate had an unpleasant feeling in her stomach.

It was one thing to cross out the ones who stood by your side, but it was more of a problem when he placed fear in the hearts of Tipton's crew. He knew a feasible plan was needed, or their business would crash on everyone's head.

"Dejuan, is not the person he's pretending to be, he's soft. I wouldn't give a damn how many people that nigga shot. Right now, we've been moving this product at a pace that's gon' have us rich in the next year. To prevent us all from falling and losing everything we worked so hard to build. I'ma put a ticket on that boy's head. I tried to refrain from sliding that nigga off the face of the earth. Nothing needs to be traced back to us. It only takes someone to give these people a hint that we touched that boy and we're all gone." Tipton tried to make them see the entire picture.

"I'll take care of him, God." Halo stood by the kitchen entrance.

"No, you're not a fucking flunkie bro. You're my killer, but that don't mean your face will be put on every problem that pops up. Eventually, someone will see you and try to be a hero. That's gonna send you back to prison faster than you can blink. All y'all have to understand this. We have a major drug operation going on, right now. Doing anything to make ourselves visible could get us put behind a wall for the rest of our lives. I got, Dejaun. We just need more security on the team."

"I still got my two young goons. Them lil' niggas will tear the city apart if you tell them too. They're just too hot. I don't wanna bring more heat to us when we're already trying to keep our head above water with this bullshit," Rex said lighting a blunt.

"Right now, we don't have a choice. Pay both of them to ensure more safety. Chocolate, I know you might be comfortable in this spot, but it's time to switch it up. Same thing for you, Sincere. The more we change things. The harder it is for anyone to pull grimy on us."

"Smooth." Rex pulled out his phone.

"Next week, I'm picking up a hundred. This ain't no average load. I need everyone on point. Especially you, Chocolate. I know I might not say this on the regular, but you're an important part of our business. You're my second half to this entire movement."

"Aww, I'm finally being recognized for all this good ass work. Thank you, sweetie." She wiped a fake tear from her eye.

Shaking his head with a smile, his cell phone sounded off. He stepped away from the table and entered the living room. "Waddup, who this?"

"Mr. White, this is Ms. Cornell from the rehabilitation center. I'm calling about your auntie," she informed. "Mr. White, your auntie has abandoned the facility and we are very worried. We have a small search team out to see if she can be located.

"And how did this happen?" Tipton asked.

"Well, yesterday I searched for her and noticed that she wasn't in the building. Just the day before, she told me that if I wanted to talk, I would need a co-pay or something of that nature. I know she didn't want to be here. I thought she might have found her way back to you. You're the only contact that I have on file."

Knowing the woman's words were accurate, he snapped his fingers to get Halo's attention. "I'll head out to see if I can track her down. If I find out anything, I'll be sure to let you know," he replied before hanging up.

"You a'ight?" Chocolate sensed his mood quickly changed.

"Nothing is ever a'ight, business must go on. Y'all keep that in mind. I'll be through here bright and early." Watching him leave out the front door with Halo on his tail, Rex pondered before picking up his phone.

Chris Green

Chapter 24

The flashes of the blue and red police lights sparkled in his eyes, as he stood in front of Lisa's home. Officers flooded the area, while the nearby neighbors were posted on the sideline whispering about the discovered tragedy. The sight of his auntie's dead body gave him the same chills the night his mother was murdered.

"Say, kid, do you mind if I speak to you for a minute?"

Facing the woman, Tipton grew cautious after spotting the badge on her jeans. Her fluffy eyebrows and olive skin gave her the look of a retired principal who didn't mind getting you sent to prison. Her gray hair hung down to the center of her neck and the two large pistols that rested under her arms clearly showed that she wasn't a rookie.

"I'm sorry for your loss. Any ideas who would want to hurt her?"

"No, she's never had problems with anyone. I checked her into a drug center a few days ago. They just called today about her abandoning the facility. I just so happen to stop by here and found her like this." Tipton lowered his head.

"Drug center. You don't think she owed the dealer any funds do ya?"

Feeling the comment was past disrespectful, Tipton's arms folded with an angry expression. "Who the fuck are you?"

"Detective, Sandra Elliott, the one who's trying to figure out what happened to your fucking family. Refrain from the smart mouth remarks when you speak to me, young man."

"I'm sorry, but I'm lost like everyone else. This shit is hard to stomach."

"That's understandable. It's also hard on my end to investigate murders for the last twenty years. All I'm trying to do is find out what happened here. I can't bring you any closure if I don't know nothing," she responded trying to coax an answer out of him.

"Ma'am, no disrespect, but it doesn't seem like you're here to commiserate me about my auntie. It looks like you wanna label me a suspect. If it's not too much to ask, please get in contact with me after you do your fucking job?" Tipton shouted before walking off.

Once he got across the street, he climbed back into his driver's seat. "What you think going on, God?" Halo looked at all the unmarked cars.

His cell began to ring before he could reply. He shook his head in disbelief, pulled it out and answered. "Who this?"

"Nigga, you can't greet your pops better than that?" Vel spoke through the line.

Glancing at the screen, Tipton placed the phone back up to his ear. "How the fuck did you get my number?"

"I got my resources. Try and calm your tone down because I didn't call to argue with you like a bitch. I just wanna ask a question?"

"And you must can't understand English bitch ass nigga? What part of me not fucking with you ain't clicking? You ain't my fucking pops. So, I'll ask again, why you calling my line?"

"I guess you a killer now, huh?" Vel chuckled.

"Only one way to see." Tipton tested his gangsta.

"That's cool, I'ma break something down to you like this. I asked you to run with me and get this loot. I gave you the proposition of a lifetime and yo' dumbass acted like I offered you a job shoveling shit. Since we can't compromise like family, I'll give you a choice. Either come in with the recipe or sell your shit in another state. Pick one," Vel demanded.

"You got some real nuts faggot ass, old man. Matter fact, I can remember your address like my last name. Now let's make a deal that you can't refuse. Try yo' best to stay out of my way or I'm going to start making funeral arrangements for you." Tipton ended the call.

"We might need to handle something." He glanced over at Halo before pulling away.

Shit was beautiful and all was well until Vel stepped in his path. Mr. Bishop's words floated in his mind while pushing the dash to reach the expressway.

"Everything a'ight, God?"

"I'm starting not to know anymore," he said, as they pulled up to the red traffic light.

"We don't stress over problems, God. Remember?" Halo reminded him.

Hearing the loud music that blared out next to them, Tipton looked to his left and met eyes with Dejuan sitting in the driver's seat of the Cadillac truck. The back window rolled down, he flashed a crooked smile, as Skeet aimed his two pistols directly for him and Halo.

"Duck!" That was all Tipton got a chance to scream before a bundle of bullets started flying.

Boc! Boc! Boc! Boc! Boc! Boc!

To Be Continued...
Dope Boy Magic 2
Coming Soon!

Submission Guideline

Submit the first three chapters of your completed manuscript to ldpsubmissions@gmail.com, subject line: Your book's title. The manuscript must be in a .doc file and sent as an attachment. Document should be in Times New Roman, double spaced and in size 12 font. Also, provide your synopsis and full contact information. If sending multiple submissions, they must each be in a separate email.

Have a story but no way to send it electronically? You can still submit to LDP/Ca$h Presents. Send in the first three chapters, written or typed, of your completed manuscript to:

LDP: Submissions Dept
Po Box 870494
Mesquite, Tx 75187

DO NOT send original manuscript. Must be a duplicate.

Provide your synopsis and a cover letter containing your full contact information.

Thanks for considering LDP and Ca$h Presents.

Coming Soon from Lock Down Publications/Ca$h Presents

BOW DOWN TO MY GANGSTA

By **Ca$h**

TORN BETWEEN TWO

By **Coffee**

BLOOD STAINS OF A SHOTTA **III**

By **Jamaica**

STEADY MOBBIN **III**

By **Marcellus Allen**

BLOOD OF A BOSS **VI**

SHADOWS OF THE GAME II

By **Askari**

LOYAL TO THE GAME **IV**

By **T.J. & Jelissa**

A DOPEBOY'S PRAYER **II**

By **Eddie "Wolf" Lee**

IF LOVING YOU IS WRONG… **III**

By **Jelissa**

TRUE SAVAGE **VII**

MIDNIGHT CARTEL

DOPE BOY MAGIC II

By **Chris Green**

BLAST FOR ME **III**

DUFFLE BAG CARTEL **IV**

HEARTLESS GOON **III**

A SAVAGE DOPEBOY II

DRUG LORDS II

By **Ghost**

Chris Green

A HUSTLER'S DECEIT III

KILL ZONE **II**

BAE BELONGS TO ME III

SOUL OF A MONSTER III

By **Aryanna**

THE COST OF LOYALTY **III**

By **Kweli**

THE SAVAGE LIFE III

By **J-Blunt**

KING OF NEW YORK V

COKE KINGS IV

BORN HEARTLESS III

By **T.J. Edwards**

GORILLAZ IN THE BAY V

De'Kari

THE STREETS ARE CALLING II

Duquie Wilson

KINGPIN KILLAZ IV

STREET KINGS III

PAID IN BLOOD III

CARTEL KILLAZ III

Hood Rich

SINS OF A HUSTLA II

ASAD

TRIGGADALE III

Elijah R. Freeman

KINGZ OF THE GAME V

Playa Ray

SLAUGHTER GANG IV

RUTHLESS HEART II

By Willie Slaughter

THE HEART OF A SAVAGE II

By Jibril Williams

FUK SHYT II

By Blakk Diamond

THE DOPEMAN'S BODYGAURD II

By Tranay Adams

TRAP GOD II

By Troublesome

YAYO II

A SHOOTER'S AMBITION II

By S. Allen

GHOST MOB

Stilloan Robinson

KINGPIN DREAMS

By Paper Boi Rari

CREAM

By Yolanda Moore

SON OF A DOPE FIEND II

By Renta

FOREVER GANGSTA II

By Adrian Dulan

LOYALTY AIN'T PROMISED

By Keith Williams

THE PRICE YOU PAY FOR LOVE

By Destiny Skai

THE LIFE OF A HOOD STAR

By Rashia Wilson

Chris Green

TOE TAGZ II
By Ah'Million

<u>Available Now</u>

RESTRAINING ORDER **I & II**
By **CA$H & Coffee**
LOVE KNOWS NO BOUNDARIES **I II & III**
By **Coffee**
RAISED AS A GOON I, II, III & IV
BRED BY THE SLUMS I, II, III
BLAST FOR ME I & II
ROTTEN TO THE CORE I II III
A BRONX TALE I, II, III
DUFFEL BAG CARTEL I II III
HEARTLESS GOON
A SAVAGE DOPEBOY
HEARTLESS GOON I II
DRUG LORDS
By **Ghost**
LAY IT DOWN **I & II**
LAST OF A DYING BREED
BLOOD STAINS OF A SHOTTA I & II
By **Jamaica**
LOYAL TO THE GAME
LOYAL TO THE GAME II
LOYAL TO THE GAME III
LIFE OF SIN I, II III
By **TJ & Jelissa**

BLOODY COMMAS I & II

SKI MASK CARTEL I II & III

KING OF NEW YORK I II,III IV

RISE TO POWER I II III

COKE KINGS I II III

BORN HEARTLESS I II

By **T.J. Edwards**

IF LOVING HIM IS WRONG…I & II

LOVE ME EVEN WHEN IT HURTS I II III

By **Jelissa**

WHEN THE STREETS CLAP BACK I & II III

By **Jibril Williams**

A DISTINGUISHED THUG STOLE MY HEART I II & III

LOVE SHOULDN'T HURT I II III IV

RENEGADE BOYS I II III IV

By **Meesha**

A GANGSTER'S CODE I &, II III

A GANGSTER'S SYN I II III

THE SAVAGE LIFE I II

By **J-Blunt**

PUSH IT TO THE LIMIT

By **Bre' Hayes**

BLOOD OF A BOSS **I, II, III, IV, V**

SHADOWS OF THE GAME

By **Askari**

THE STREETS BLEED MURDER **I, II & III**

THE HEART OF A GANGSTA I II& III

By **Jerry Jackson**

CUM FOR ME

CUM FOR ME 2

CUM FOR ME 3

CUM FOR ME 4

CUM FOR ME 5

An **LDP Erotica Collaboration**

BRIDE OF A HUSTLA **I II & II**

THE FETTI GIRLS **I, II& III**

CORRUPTED BY A GANGSTA I, II III, IV

BLINDED BY HIS LOVE

By **Destiny Skai**

WHEN A GOOD GIRL GOES BAD

By **Adrienne**

THE COST OF LOYALTY I II

By Kweli

A GANGSTER'S REVENGE **I II III & IV**

THE BOSS MAN'S DAUGHTERS

THE BOSS MAN'S DAUGHTERS II

THE BOSSMAN'S DAUGHTERS III

THE BOSSMAN'S DAUGHTERS IV

THE BOSS MAN'S DAUGHTERS **V**

A SAVAGE LOVE **I & II**

BAE BELONGS TO ME I II

A HUSTLER'S DECEIT I, II, III

WHAT BAD BITCHES DO I, II, III

SOUL OF A MONSTER I II

KILL ZONE

By **Aryanna**

A KINGPIN'S AMBITON

A KINGPIN'S AMBITION **II**

I MURDER FOR THE DOUGH

By **Ambitious**

TRUE SAVAGE

TRUE SAVAGE II

TRUE SAVAGE **III**

TRUE SAVAGE **IV**

TRUE SAVAGE **V**

TRUE SAVAGE **VI**

DOPE BOY MAGIC

By **Chris Green**

A DOPEBOY'S PRAYER

By **Eddie "Wolf" Lee**

THE KING CARTEL **I, II & III**

By **Frank Gresham**

THESE NIGGAS AIN'T LOYAL **I, II & III**

By **Nikki Tee**

GANGSTA SHYT **I II &III**

By **CATO**

THE ULTIMATE BETRAYAL

By **Phoenix**

BOSS'N UP **I , II & III**

By **Royal Nicole**

I LOVE YOU TO DEATH

By Destiny J

I RIDE FOR MY HITTA

I STILL RIDE FOR MY HITTA

By **Misty Holt**

LOVE & CHASIN' PAPER

By **Qay Crockett**

TO DIE IN VAIN

SINS OF A HUSTLA

By **ASAD**

BROOKLYN HUSTLAZ

By **Boogsy Morina**

BROOKLYN ON LOCK I & II

By **Sonovia**

GANGSTA CITY

By **Teddy Duke**

A DRUG KING AND HIS DIAMOND I & II III

A DOPEMAN'S RICHES

HER MAN, MINE'S TOO I, II

CASH MONEY HO'S

By Nicole Goosby

TRAPHOUSE KING **I II & III**

KINGPIN KILLAZ I II III

STREET KINGS I II

PAID IN BLOOD **I II**

CARTEL KILLAZ I II

By **Hood Rich**

LIPSTICK KILLAH **I, II, III**

CRIME OF PASSION I II & III

By **Mimi**

STEADY MOBBN' **I, II, III**

By **Marcellus Allen**

WHO SHOT YA **I, II, III**

SON OF A DOPE FIEND

Renta

GORILLAZ IN THE BAY **I II III IV**

Dope Boy Magic

DE'KARI

TRIGGADALE I II

Elijah R. Freeman

GOD BLESS THE TRAPPERS I, II, III

THESE SCANDALOUS STREETS I, II, III

FEAR MY GANGSTA I, II, III

THESE STREETS DON'T LOVE NOBODY I, II

BURY ME A G I, II, III, IV, V

A GANGSTA'S EMPIRE I, II, III, IV

THE DOPEMAN'S BODYGAURD

Tranay Adams

THE STREETS ARE CALLING

Duquie Wilson

MARRIED TO A BOSS… I II III

By Destiny Skai & Chris Green

KINGZ OF THE GAME I II III IV

Playa Ray

SLAUGHTER GANG I II III

RUTHLESS HEART

By Willie Slaughter

THE HEART OF A SAVAGE

By Jibril Williams

FUK SHYT

By Blakk Diamond

DON'T F#CK WITH MY HEART I II

By Linnea

ADDICTED TO THE DRAMA I II III

By Jamila

YAYO

189

A SHOOTER'S AMBITION

By S. Allen

TRAP GOD

By Troublesome

FOREVER GANGSTA

By Adrian Dulan

TOE TAGZ

By Ah'Million

BOOKS BY LDP'S CEO, CA$H

TRUST IN NO MAN

TRUST IN NO MAN 2

TRUST IN NO MAN 3

BONDED BY BLOOD

SHORTY GOT A THUG

THUGS CRY

THUGS CRY 2

THUGS CRY 3

TRUST NO BITCH

TRUST NO BITCH 2

TRUST NO BITCH 3

TIL MY CASKET DROPS

RESTRAINING ORDER

RESTRAINING ORDER 2

IN LOVE WITH A CONVICT

Coming Soon

BONDED BY BLOOD 2

BOW DOWN TO MY GANGSTA

Chris Green